POWER PLAY

BY ERIC WALTERS

HarperCollins*Publishers*Ltd

Power Play
Copyright © 2013 by Eric Walters.
Afterword © 2013 by Sheldon Kennedy.
All rights reserved.

Published by HarperCollins Publishers Ltd.

First edition.

HarperCollins books may be purchased for educational, business, or sales
promotional use through our Special Markets Department.

HarperCollins Publishers Ltd.
2 Bloor Street East, 20th Floor
Toronto, Ontario, Canada
M4W 1A8

www.harpercollins.ca

Library and Archives Canada Cataloguing in Publication data
is available upon request.

ISBN 978-1-44340-761-8

Printed and bound in the United States

RRD 9 8 7 6 5 4 3 2 1

For those with the strength to speak up—
and those who are willing to help.

POWER PLAY

CHAPTER ONE

The big gate at the end of the rink opened up and the Zamboni slowed down and then exited. I jumped on the ice and felt an instant jolt of joy. My skates felt like they were gliding *above* it, like I was flying on a cloud, and for a brief second the ice was all mine. A perfect surface, unmarked, ready for me, just for me. It felt as wonderful now as it did when I was a kid playing for fun. It was still fun, but it was more than just playing around now.

Of course, that feeling didn't last more than a split second as my teammates piled on behind me, and coming from the other side, our opponents. Our enemies. I couldn't make out their faces beneath the helmets and cages. That was probably better. If you could see faces, you might mistake them for *people*. I couldn't afford to see them that way. Until the game was done, I actually *hated* them, and really, the final buzzer didn't soften the hate that much. They were standing in my way, in the way of my teammates and what we wanted, and I was prepared to do whatever was necessary to get it.

I took my turn extra wide, drifting well over centre ice into their end of the rink. I knew I wasn't supposed to, but I did it anyway. As I made my pass through their territory, a couple of them got out of my way. Cowards. They knew that if any opponent dared to drift over to our side, I'd hit him so hard his head would spin.

The refs wouldn't have even noticed. They were standing off to the side, too busy chatting and trying to impress each other. There was no one else in the whole arena they could even hope to impress. People who *couldn't* play hockey became refs so they could take it out on all those players who were better than them.

I hated refs almost as much as I hated the players on the other side. Except for the uniforms, there often wasn't much to tell one from the other. Was there ever a game when the refs didn't have it in for me and my team?

I scanned the stands for my mother. There wasn't much of a crowd so it was easy enough to pick her out, in the corner, by herself, away from the other parents, where she usually sat. My father was nowhere to be seen. No surprise there either. When he did come, it was never for the warm-ups and seldom for the first period. That would have cut seriously into his pre-game drinking time. There was a legion hall next door to this arena where you could get a drink. I could even picture the table he was sitting at, talking to the veterans, slapping backs, shaking hands, and even buying the occasional beer for somebody. He was the life of the party. Unfortunately, life with him was no party. Well, at least he couldn't embarrass me as long as he was sitting in a bar. But the later he arrived, the more time he'd had to drink, the more likely there'd be trouble when he did show up.

His voice could cut through the arena like a knife. Rough and raw and loud and laced with enough swear words to get everybody's attention. My father would take aim at anybody. He would ride the refs, the guys on the other team, a parent, even my teammates. And me. Lots of times it was me.

The way they reacted, it was clear that a lot of people in the stands were more than a little afraid of him. And I heard some parent once mutter something about "fruit not falling far from the tree." Screw them. I was *nothing* like him.

The year before, he'd got into it with another parent in the stands, and he was banned from the arena for two months. That was the easiest two months of hockey I ever played.

No time to worry about him now, though. I had to warm up and think about the game. I took a pass on the tape, right in the sweet spot, pumped my legs a few strides, then glided toward our goalie. His five-hole was open, as always. No matter how many times he'd been told that was his weakness, he didn't seem to be able to fix it. It would have been too easy to just shoot there so I picked a corner—glove side. I put a small fake to my left then snapped it up, the mesh popping out as the puck hit the back.

"Nice try," I mumbled as I skated by. That was a better thing to say to your goalie than "Can't you stop anything?" which is what I really felt like yelling.

Despite the fact that our goalie couldn't stop a bowling ball, I still felt a little rush of adrenalin and happiness when the puck hit the twine. It didn't matter if it was in the warm-ups, a game, or just shooting into a net in my driveway by myself—scoring still gave me that rush. I was addicted to that feeling.

That first shot was for *my* warm-up. The next few I'd deliberately shoot into his pads. It was more important to pump up his confidence than it was for me to score. I *knew* I could score—he *didn't* know if he could stop. Confidence was important, especially for a goalie. They were strange guys, and you had to make sure they didn't get too down on themselves before the game even started. I hated to admit it, but we needed him. It wouldn't matter how much rubber I got by the other goalie if ours couldn't stop their shots.

I skated right up to centre and stopped, looking over our opposition. They were good. Second in the league. We were in fifth, on the bubble of making the playoffs. We needed this win more than they did. I didn't think they had that much more talent than we did, but they seemed to be getting all the breaks. And having the "C" on my sweater meant that I had to make those breaks happen for us. It was up to me to carry the team on my back.

I scowled at each guy on the other team as they skated by. Most of them looked away, not meeting my eyes. The game started long before the puck was dropped and didn't end when the whistle blew. Just like I had to boost up my teammates, I had to get under the skin of the guys on the other side. There was a saying: "If you can't beat 'em in the alley, you can't beat 'em on the ice." I wasn't the biggest guy, but everybody knew that I was ready to drop my gloves with anybody, any time, and even if I didn't come out the winner, the other guy would for sure know he'd been in a fight. Sometimes it was worth the automatic suspension.

The warm-ups continued until Coach called us over. Most of the guys climbed onto the bench along with him while six of us—our goalie and the starting five—stood on the ice along with a few other skaters. There was no need for Coach to tell us who were the starters—we all knew.

"This is an important game," Coach began, "not just for us as a team, but for specific members of the team too."

What exactly did that mean?

"I've been told that there is going to be a very important scout in the crowd. He's come here to look at a number of players in this game who might be drafted into Junior A next year."

There was a buzz as everybody started talking at once. They all thought the scout would be looking at only four or five players. And each of them—no matter how bad they really were—figured they were one of those four or five players. And if they weren't, it didn't matter—if they had the game of their lives, they figured it might be just enough to get them on his radar and drafted. Idiots. Did they really think one game would be enough?

I *was* one of those players he'd come to look at. Everybody knew that.

"And while I want you to play extra hard, I want you all to pretend he isn't here," Coach continued.

Wouldn't it have been easier if he just hadn't said anything to begin with? Now every player would try to impress the scout by doing things that he really wasn't capable of doing. And worst of all, those with the least talent would be working the hardest to impress him. Instead, they'd just screw up.

The ref blew his whistle.

"Go out and get 'em!" Coach yelled.

I skated toward centre ice. My mom gave me a little wave from the bleachers and I nodded back. There was no point even looking for the scout. It didn't matter if I could see him or not. The important thing was that he saw me, and I was going to make it impossible for him to miss me. I didn't care if he'd come here to see ten players. He was only going to notice one for sure. Me.

CHAPTER TWO

I smashed my stick against the boards as our goalie dug the puck out of our net—again. With less than two minutes left in the game that pretty well sealed our loss. They were up by three—5–2. I'd done my best, scoring one goal and setting up the second. And I'd delivered hits on anything that moved, except the officials. But even though we'd outshot them, I couldn't stop the puck from going in our net. Why didn't we have a *real* goalie?

I skated toward centre and looked to where my mother and father were sitting. My father had arrived just before the end of the second period, his voice cutting through the noise of the rink and lodging right in my head. It sounded like he was only half in the bag, and at least his anger was directed toward the refs tonight and not me. I had to be grateful for the small stuff, although I was still going to catch it from him on the ride home for the dozens of things I'd either done wrong or failed to do to begin with. My father always droned on about how hockey was a team game—unless we lost, and then it was all my fault.

I lined up for the face-off. The player opposite me was from their fourth line—probably the worst player on their team. No skills, but lots of size. He towered over me. Their coach putting him out against me in the final minutes of a game that was already decided could mean only one thing. This was payback for a couple of hits I'd put on his star players.

"You've lost another one," he said with a scowl plastered on his face. "Your team sucks."

No argument there—especially if he was referring to our goalie.

"How does it feel to be a loser?" he asked.

Again, I didn't answer.

"What's wrong?" he asked. "You spend the whole game mouthing off and now you got nothing to say?"

"You're right," I said.

He looked surprised. I guess being right was a new experience for him.

"The game *must* be over if they put a *goon* like you out here."

"What did you say?" he demanded.

"I'm agreeing with you. The game *is* over." I pointed toward the scoreboard.

He glanced up, and in that split second, I dropped my stick and gloves and landed two blows to his jaw! He went down like he'd been shot, and then I was bowled over by another player and everybody on the ice was pairing off!

• • •

The lineman steered me off to the gate leading to the dressing room. I struggled with him, but only a little. Going too easily would have shown that I wanted to leave the ice, and fighting too hard would have got me a suspension. Besides, I was busy yelling at the last guy I'd exchanged blows with. I could taste the damage that he'd done to me. I spat, and red stained the ice.

I'd got two minutes for instigating, a five-minute fighting major, and a ten-minute misconduct because I wouldn't stop trying to get at one of their players. With so little time left in the game, the automatic ejection didn't mean much, but I knew there'd be at least a one-game suspension to go with it.

"Don't come back on!" the ref said as I stepped off the ice. "If you do, I'll make it my personal business to make sure you get a five-game suspension."

I mumbled a couple of swear words at him, but he didn't need to threaten me. I was just as glad to spend the last few minutes of the game in the dressing room instead of watching the other team congratulate each other as we skated off with our tails between our legs.

One of my teammates brought over my stick and gloves and helmet.

"Way to handle yourself, Cody," he said.

"You did okay too, man."

He gave me a big smile. He hadn't done badly. He had my back when a third guy jumped me, pulling him off. I wouldn't forget that. I'd have his back the next time something exploded.

"We'll get 'em the next time," he said.

"Unless we win the next few games, we won't get to play them again."

"Maybe not, but even if we didn't win the game, they'll remember who won the fight."

He was right about that.

I started down the tunnel toward the dressing room—then hesitated. Disappearing into the dressing room would be like hiding, like they'd scared me off or chased me away. That wasn't going to happen.

I turned around and went back out to where I could see the game, standing in the passageway. I wanted everybody to be able to see me, to know that they could toss me out of the game but they couldn't toss me very far. I'd be watching, taking names and numbers for the next time we met, even if it was next season.

The play was down in our end—they had a power play because I'd gotten the instigator penalty. I just hoped they wouldn't score, although, really, what did it matter? Lose by three or lose by thirty, it was still a loss.

I looked up toward my parents. A man had walked over to where they were sitting. He was wearing a suit—which meant he wasn't a friend of my father's. Was he the scout? I'd tried to put him out of my mind, but it would have been better for him to see a win instead of a loss. It was my team, and I was the captain. A real leader would have dragged his team to victory.

Mercifully, the power play ended, and then the game, without any more scoring. I opened up the gate, and as my teammates came over, I gave each a tap on the butt and told him "Good game," "Way to play," "Sometimes the best team doesn't win," or whatever I thought he needed to hear.

Some of the guys looked like their dog had died. Others were joking and acting like a hot girl had invited them over when her parents weren't home. I had to fight the urge to reach out and smack those smiles off their faces. If losing didn't matter, then neither did winning, so why even show up to begin with? They kept score for a reason. My father had once said to me, "Show me a good loser, and I'll show you a loser." I hated being a loser.

Coach was the last one off, slipping along the ice.

"You played a good game, Cody," he said.

"Not good enough."

"It's a team sport and you did more than your part." He paused. "Come on, nobody died out there, although that one guy you decked at the end might feel like he's close to it. Somebody might want to check to see if there's a toe tag attached!"

"Maybe he'll keep his mouth shut the next time."

Coach gave me a slap on the back. "Maybe we would have done better if you'd smacked somebody earlier."

I nodded. "I'll remember that for next game."

I *had* done well, and it *was* a team sport, and I knew that nobody had died out there . . . but still, shouldn't the coach have been a bit more upset about losing? He was a nice guy, but he wasn't really much of a coach. After our goalie, he was the second-biggest liability on the team. Nice guys finished last . . . or at least in fifth place.

I trod down the rubber mat, following him to the dressing room. I knew he'd give us a cheery little speech and then release us to our waiting parents. Then, on the drive home, I'd be exposed to my father's not-so-cheery, not-so-little speech. If I was lucky, he'd be gone already, either back at the bar or driving home without me. He did that sometimes when he thought I hadn't played very well. Some punishment. Being away from him was a reward. Besides, it wasn't that long a walk from home games. And if it was an away game, a bus ride or even a very, very long walk was worth not having to listen to his half-baked, half-drunk ranting. Sometimes he took my mother along. Other times she stayed and walked with me or took the bus.

I thought back to that man sitting with my parents at the end of the game. It had to be the scout. I just hoped that my father hadn't said anything to him that would screw things up . . . assuming losing the game hadn't been bad enough.

CHAPTER THREE

I threw all my equipment into my hockey bag and grabbed my stick. I could tell by the sound it made when I tapped it against the concrete floor that it had a little crack. Must have happened when I hit it against the boards after that last goal against us. It was now useless, but I couldn't throw it away; I didn't know if I could get another one before the next game. Sticks are expensive. But as long as I showed up with a stick for the next game and then "broke" it during the warm-ups, I could count on somebody to "loan" me one. Funny how there always seemed to be enough money for beer in my house but not for other things.

I shouted out my goodbyes and left the dressing room. My mother was standing in the corridor, by herself. I guess my father had left both of us behind this time. At least I'd have company on the walk home. Other parents, standing in clusters, were waiting for their kids to appear. Some were just happy that their kid hadn't got hurt, and they didn't really care if we'd won or lost. Others took the game as seriously as my father did—as seriously as I did. They'd probably dreamt about getting to the NHL themselves, or dreamt now that their kid would get there. I guess it was good to have a dream, but for most of them it was about time they woke up to reality.

My mother gave me a quick hug. "Your father is waiting."

"Oh." I was pleased and displeased all at once. I wouldn't have to walk, but I would have to listen.

"He's next door at the legion having a drink," she said.

Great. Now he was going to talk *and* drive with another drink in him.

"He's with a scout."

"The scout!" I exclaimed.

"He came over and talked to us at the end of the game. Let's hurry," she said. "It's not good to keep him waiting."

I saw that anxious look in her eyes. Living with my father was like living on the side of a volcano. Even when it hadn't erupted for a long time, you still lived in fear that it might blow any day.

My mother took my stick and we moved quickly through the arena, going out through one of the side exits and into the parking lot. The legion hall was just across the way.

"Does it hurt?" she asked.

"Does what hurt?"

She pointed at my nose.

"Not really."

"It looks sore."

"It isn't. I'd forgotten all about it until you mentioned it."

That was only partially a lie. My nose was throbbing, but it didn't actually hurt. I had really high pain tolerance, especially during a game. When I was playing, it was like I could turn pain off. A blocked shot, a slash, even a hit into the boards never seemed to hurt until long after the game was over. It was almost as if I could detach my mind from my body.

We walked into the legion. My father loved legions, and there seemed to be one close to every arena. They all seemed the same: worn wooden tables and chairs, dim lighting, flags and pictures of veterans in uniform lining the walls, and still, unmoving air that smelled like stale beer.

I could hear my father before I could see him. His voice filled the room, which was almost empty except for a table of old-timers sitting in the corner, nursing their beers and playing cards. He waved us over. The man in the suit—the scout—got to his feet. He was big—more fat than muscular—but seemed friendly as he greeted us with a big smile and an extended hand.

"Hello, Cody, good to meet you," he said. "I'm Mr. Connors."

"Good to meet you, sir." I shook his hand.

"Sir?" he said and smiled. "Nice to see a young man with manners."

"I raised him right," my father said. "I always told him to show manners or get a swat." He mimicked a hit to the back of my head but stopped just short of actually making contact. I made sure not to flinch.

"Hopefully you didn't have to swat him very often," Mr. Connors said.

"The kid is not a quick learner. Thank goodness there's not much up there to hurt," my father said. He laughed that harsh, raspy, too-much-to-drink-and-smoke laugh of his.

"He certainly seemed pretty smart out there on the ice," Mr. Connors said. "He has great hockey IQ."

I was glad he could see that. I did know hockey.

"Smart on the ice, yes. At school, not so much," my father said.

Mr. Connors looked concerned. "Is school a problem, Cody?"

"Not a problem," I said. "I just don't like it very much."

"School is important," he said. "*Very* important." He paused. "But I'm here to talk about hockey. You did well out there today."

"We didn't win."

"And that bothers you," he said.

"That bothers me a lot. I don't play to lose."

"I appreciate the attitude. Individual stats don't matter if the team loses, but regardless, you played well. You got yourself a Gordie Howe hat trick."

"What?" I questioned.

"You know who Gordie Howe is, right?" he asked.

"Of course he does!" my father exclaimed.

"I just don't get the hat trick part . . . I only scored one goal."

"One goal, one assist, and one fight. That's a Gordie Howe hat trick," he explained.

"Now there was a *player*," my father thundered. "He could beat you with a goal, beat you with a blocked shot, or just plain beat you . . . one punch!" He smacked his hand against the table, rattling the glasses of beer. The one in front of Mr. Connors sloshed onto the table. "He retired with eight hundred and one regular-season goals. Best player the game has ever seen."

"Wouldn't that be Gretzky—eight hundred and ninety four regular-season goals?" I asked.

"Gretzky!" my father said with disdain. "He wouldn't have lasted a season back in the Original Six! No helmets, no face guards, no goalie masks. And a player was supposed to take care of himself, nobody there to babysit him and be his bodyguard. Howe didn't need a bodyguard."

"Gordie was as tough as nails," Mr. Connor agreed. "Your father was telling me about his own days in Senior A."

No surprise there. He told everybody about his glory days, especially when he'd been drinking, which was most of the time.

"I guess you've heard some of the stories," Mr. Connors said to me.

I almost laughed out loud, but just nodded my head in agreement. I'd heard all of them dozens of times—and they often had different endings. At least when he changed the story it made it more interesting.

"That wasn't hockey back then as much as it was *war*!" my father exclaimed.

"Those were the days. I wish I could have been around to see some of those games," Mr. Connors said.

"I *was* there," my father said. "I had the speed, I had the hands, and I had the game. The way I played would make this one look like a figure skater," he said, gesturing to me.

I could always count on him for the compliments.

"The only break I ever got was the wrong kind— snapped my leg in two." He shook his head slowly. "Never the same after that."

"I've seen it before," Mr. Connors said. "Not just an injury ending a career but somebody who could have had a shot at the bigs never getting that shot. And that doesn't even count the politics around the game."

"Don't get me started on that one," my father agreed.

"Sometimes it isn't what you can *do*, but who you *know*," Mr. Connors said.

"You listening to this?" said my father, leaning across the table to give me a tap on the arm.

"I'm listening."

"And is that your dream?" Mr. Connors asked me. "To make it to the Show?"

"Isn't that everybody's dream?"

"For most, that's all it is. They aren't prepared to do what it takes, to wake up and do the work."

"I would have done anything," my father said.

"Sometimes it's a son's destiny to live his father's dreams," Mr. Connors said.

"Him?" my father asked. "You think *he* could make it to the NHL?"

"No one can guarantee anything, but Cody has potential. There's only one question." He turned directly to me. "How much do you want it?"

"Bad."

"How bad?" he asked.

"Really bad."

"And what would you be prepared to do to get there?" Mr. Connors asked.

"He'd do whatever it takes," my father said, answering for me. "We'd all be prepared to do whatever needs to be done."

"I've seen lots of people with talent who weren't prepared to make the sacrifices," the scout said. "I'll give you an example. Cody, do you have a girlfriend?"

"Um . . . not really."

"Good! One of the biggest distractions, one of the things that drains focus, is having a girlfriend."

"Women," my father said, shaking his head. "You know what they say: 'A man isn't complete until he's married . . . and then he's *finished*!'"

My mother smiled weakly as my father laughed loudly. He was always the best audience for his own jokes.

"You married?" my father asked Mr. Connors.

"Only to the game. But she will demand a lot from you if you want to be the best. Cody, do you want to be the best?"

"Yes, sir."

"No hesitation. I believe you. You have the heart and you have the toughness, but you have to work on improving your skills. You've never been to any development camps, have you?"

"No, sir."

"Why not?" he asked.

I was embarrassed to tell him. I guess my father wasn't.

"Too much money!" he said.

"Some of them offer scholarships to deserving people," Mr. Connors said. "Like the one I run. I'm allowed to fill two spaces each session without charge. Would you be interested in attending camp?"

"You'd do that for me?" I asked.

"I would, because I believe you just might have what it takes."

"That's incredible . . . thank you so much . . . I don't know what to say."

"Just say yes. And there's no telling what might happen after that. After watching you play, talking to you and your parents, I think I'm going to recommend you be given serious consideration in the Junior A draft."

Now I was speechless. Junior A was only one step away, and the NHL was just one step up from there.

"I'll send you all the details," Mr. Connors said. "But first things first." He reached into his pocket. "These are for you," he said, handing something to my father.

My father looked at them and his eyes widened in shock. "These are platinum seats! For this Saturday's game between the Leafs and the Bruins!"

"I get tickets all the time, and I thought you'd be the sort of person who would really enjoy and appreciate a battle between two of the Original Six," Mr. Connors explained.

"Incredible! My buddy Sid's not going to believe it until me and him have our butts in those seats."

For a split second I'd actually thought he would take my mother, or even me. I should have known better, but Mr. Connors didn't. He looked at me, and we saw the hurt and surprise in each other's expressions.

"Don't worry, there will be other tickets," he said directly to me. "Count on it."

He said it with such confidence. There was something about him that made me feel like I *could* count on it. Of course, giving me more tickets might just mean my father going to more games.

"Can I see your stick?" he asked.

I picked it up off the floor, where my mother had put it down, and handed it to him.

He pressed the blade against the floor. "Nice stick . . . a bit worn. Walk me out to my car. I have a couple in the trunk. You can have them."

"Really?"

"A craftsman is only as good as his tools," he said. "But you have to make me a promise."

"Just tell me what."

"You have to promise me you'll get at least five goals out of each blade before you smash it against the boards."

I felt embarrassed.

"There's nothing to be embarrassed about," he said.

It was like he was reading my mind!

"A great coach can teach lots of things, but he can't teach passion. I'm a sucker for passion, and I can't stomach players being passive about losing. Show me a good loser—"

"And I'll show you a loser," I said, finishing his sentence.

"Exactly!" He flashed a big smile. "I like this kid," he said to my parents. He stood up. "Nice to meet you both." He shook hands with my mother and then my father.

"Great to meet you too," my father said as he held onto his hand. "You're not kidding, are you? You think the kid has a shot?"

"I've been coaching and scouting for a long time. I know my hockey. Once you get to know me, you'll see I never lie to anybody. You're not doubting me, are you?"

"Of course not!" my father exclaimed. "I can tell a man I can trust a mile away!"

"And how about you? Any doubts?" he asked me.

"No, sir."

"Excellent. Come on out and we'll get you those sticks."

I trailed after him like it was my birthday and Christmas and the last day of school all rolled into one. As we walked through the parking lot, I spotted the car that I figured was probably his—a black Escalade, parked by itself. We walked toward it.

"I was surprised that your father didn't offer to take *you* to the game," he said.

"I wasn't . . . not really."

"Too bad. You and him aren't that close."

I shook my head.

He opened up the trunk of the Escalade and pulled out two sticks—sticks that were worth a couple of hundred dollars—and handed them to me.

"Thanks . . . thanks so much," I said.

"No problem. You know, success is about a whole lot more than just the skills somebody brings to the rink."

"I know that."

"It has to do with passion, drive, who a guy is, and even where he came from—his family."

Oh great, he was going to judge me by my old man.

"It was important for me to talk to your parents," he said. "I have to know who they are, and if they're going to be part of the plan or get in the way."

"My parents really want me to make it," I said.

"I can tell."

For the first time in my life, my father had managed to make the right impression. This was even more miraculous than the sticks I was holding in my hands.

"This could be just the start. What you said in there about doing what's necessary to make it to the Show, you meant it, right?"

"Yes, of course!"

"Good, because I can only help you if you are prepared to dig down and, most important, do what I tell you. Will you do that?"

"Yes, sir."

"Then I'm prepared to help you get that dream." He flashed a big smile and held out his hand once more. "Deal?"

"Deal."

We shook.

"You'll hear from me," he said.

He climbed into his car and started it up, and I watched as he drove away.

As soon as he disappeared I could hardly believe that what had happened had *really* happened. Was he real, this guy in an expensive suit, driving an Escalade, giving away hockey tickets and free sticks? Somebody who believed in me, somebody who thought I could make it to the Show and wanted to help me get there? But there in my hands was the proof. Two first-rate, expensive hockey sticks.

CHAPTER FOUR

Stay still," my mother pleaded as she fixed my tie. She tightened it around my neck. "There, that looks really nice."

"Thanks."

"You know, you're going to have to learn to tie your own tie someday," she said.

"I hope that day is soon." All Junior A teams had game-day dress codes that included a tie and jacket and dress pants.

"And your father's jacket fits you very nicely," she added. "You're almost as big as him now."

I was almost as tall and we were about the same weight, although it was in different places—his was around his stomach and mine around the shoulders and arms. Over the past few years, I'd gotten bigger and stronger, and he'd just gotten older and fatter. I'd started to think about what would happen if the two of us ever got into it. I'd seen my father lose his temper with people on the street, at a bar, at the arena, and he could be a wild man. One of the few things that I'd inherited from him. I wondered if I could take him now. I wasn't sure, but I knew I could give him a fight. That thought was comforting and disturbing all at once.

"You don't want to keep Mr. Connors waiting," she said.

She always called him "Mr. Connors" or "Coach" when she spoke about him or to him. He was more than just a scout for Junior A, he was a really successful coach himself. Since that first meeting, he'd made regular phone calls to the house. He'd always talk to me, but he'd spend more time talking to my parents, especially my father. I could tell just from my father's side of the conversation that Coach was buttering him up. I was okay with that. Since this had all started happening, it was like my father was sort of proud of me.

"What time are you meeting Coach Connors?" my mother asked.

"The game starts at seven-thirty so we're meeting by the main entrance to the ACC at seven."

"Who's Toronto playing tonight?" she asked.

"Montreal."

"Your father would have loved to see that game."

"Coach already gave him tickets. You're the only one who still hasn't been to a game."

"That's okay," she said. "I don't even like hockey that much."

"You *don't*?"

"Well . . . I like the hockey games where my son is playing."

"In that case, then, I'm hoping you're going to see a lot of NHL games someday. And do you know what I'm going to do with my signing bonus?"

"Buy a fancy car?" she asked.

"Buy a new house . . . for you."

She smiled. "Your father would be so happy to own something nice instead of renting this sort of place . . . it would be wonderful to have something that nobody could take away from us."

"It's not for him. I'm buying the house for *you*. He can live there—as long as you want him to live with you, as long as he behaves—but it'll be *your* house."

She gave me a hug. "That is so sweet, but let's keep this our little secret."

I nodded in agreement. She was right. It was better to keep this from him, like it was important to keep lots of things from him.

"Here you go," my mother said as she handed me a twenty-dollar bill.

"Thanks a lot."

"Buy yourself a hot dog or some popcorn. It's always good to have a few dollars with you."

I stuffed the bill in my pocket. There was never a lot of extra money lying around the house, so I couldn't help but wonder if that came out of our grocery money. I guess I'd find out if we had mac and cheese more than twice this week. That wouldn't bother me. I liked mac and cheese.

• • •

I shuffled nervously from foot to foot, watching the crowd stream past the ticket takers. It was almost 7:20. I had been early, and now Coach was late and the game was going to start in ten minutes. It was tonight's game that we were going to . . . right? I looked up at the marquee— Toronto versus Montreal. Even if I'd gotten the day wrong, I wouldn't have gotten the teams wrong. Maybe he'd gotten hung up in traffic, or . . . I saw him walking through the crowd.

He was, as always, dressed in a really nice suit. Even from a distance I could tell that it was a lot fancier and more expensive than the jacket I was wearing. I felt even more out of place standing there in my father's old jacket, which smelled of cigarette smoke and spilled drinks.

Coach glided toward me. Despite the crush, it almost looked as if people were moving aside to let him by and . . . there was somebody with him. Another kid about my age . . . and he looked familiar.

Why had he brought somebody else? I'd thought this was going to be just him and me. And then I felt relieved. It was hard having to make conversation with an adult, especially one I really didn't know that well. He was nice and everything, but still.

He saw me and waved. I waved back.

"Sorry I'm a bit late," he said. "I had to pick up Josh."

Josh didn't look very comfortable either, and I wondered if the jacket he was wearing—a little too big—was *his* father's jacket too.

"Josh, this is Cody," he said.

We mumbled hellos.

"Although, you two already know each other pretty well from playing hockey against each other," Coach said.

Suddenly I recognized him: Josh Snead. I'd played against him for years. We *hated* each other.

"You broke a stick over my arm last year," he said to me.

"I'm sorry, because—" I said.

"No problem," he said, cutting me off. "It didn't hurt for that long."

"I wasn't sorry about slashing you. I was sorry because sticks are expensive. I hate to waste them."

He looked surprised . . . and then he laughed. "I gave you a few good licks after that."

We'd *danced*, with both of us getting a fighting major and me getting two for slashing, and him two for instigating. I had to give it to him—he was a scorer, not a fighter, but he hadn't backed down.

"You got in a couple of shots," I agreed. "But it wasn't me who went to the penalty box bleeding."

"Not bleeding *badly*," he protested. "I also remember I got two goals that game."

"That would explain why I broke the stick over you. We can't all get a Gordie Howe hat trick," I said.

Josh looked confused, and Coach chuckled.

"Well, I guess I got the last laugh," Josh said. "We did finish first and made it to the semifinals. Your team really tanked."

There were no gloves to drop, but if he wanted to get into it right there, that was okay with me. My hands, still at my side, were curling into fists.

"Are you two planning on having a rematch right here in the lobby?" Coach asked.

"Of course not," Josh said. "Hey, all your team really needed was a good goaltender."

I relaxed my hands. "I would have settled for one who was only half bad instead of all bad."

"Okay, gentlemen, let's get to our seats," Coach said.

• • •

I couldn't believe the seats. Platinum, a dozen rows behind the Leafs bench. We were so close that I could hear the players yelling and swearing. There are players from all over the world speaking lots of different languages on an NHL roster, but everybody seemed to speak fluent swearing. Tonight there was a lot of "communication" going on. Of course, there was no love lost between Toronto and Montreal, or the players who were on their teams.

I was a Toronto fan—frustrating because they never won anything. Being a Leafs fan meant hating everything about the Montreal Canadiens. The only thing worse than Toronto doing badly was Montreal doing well. But at least we weren't burdened by any hopes, while the Montreal fans always believed that winning was possible, even in a year like this, when they weren't any better than us. We Toronto fans *knew* we weren't going to win. Expect nothing and you don't get disappointed.

This game was, like most between these two teams, pretty close. No matter how bad Toronto was, they always seemed to save their best for Montreal. It was a 1–1 tie—which was sort of a victory for the Leafs.

The first period ended with the Leafs on a power play. Well, at least what passed for a power play. I'd given up thinking that they'd score and just hoped they wouldn't give up a short-handed goal before the period ticked off. The buzzer finally sounded.

"Anybody want anything to eat?" Coach asked. "How about a dog, a drink, and some popcorn for each of you?"

We both agreed. Coach pulled a thick wad of bills from his pocket, peeled off a couple of twenties, and handed them to Josh.

"You do the honours this time, and Cody will get 'em the next intermission."

After Josh left, sideslipping down the aisle, Coach leaned over. "Can you keep a secret?"

"No problem."

"I want to tell you something that basically nobody else *does*, or *can*, know about." He lowered his voice. "It won't be official for another two weeks, but I'm going to be named head coach of the Watertown Warriors."

"Junior A, that's amazing! Congratulations!"

"Thank you. And that has some important implications for you."

"For me?"

"I'm going to be working with the GM and the owner to determine who we're going to draft. How would you feel about playing with Watertown next year, playing for me?"

"That would be incredible!"

"Of course, that would mean moving and being billeted locally. Some kids from big cities have trouble adapting to life in a small town. And Watertown isn't just a small town, it's a hockey-crazy town. The Junior A players are local celebrities. You live under a bit of a microscope . . . everybody is watching what you do. Do you think you could handle that?"

"I'd like to try."

"What would you think of having Josh as a teammate?" Coach asked.

I didn't like him, or anybody I'd ever played against, but that wasn't the answer I was supposed to give. "He's a good player."

"He led the league in scoring," Coach said. "But you and I know that there's more to being a hockey player than scoring goals. What do you think of him as a teammate? What sort of guy do you think he'd be on the bench and in the dressing room?"

"I've never heard anything bad about him. If we're in the same dressing room, then he's my teammate."

"Good to hear. He might be worth a pick if he's still there when it's our team's turn to choose."

"I'm just not sure how he'd feel about being on the same team as me," I said. "It wasn't him that broke a stick on me. Maybe you need to ask him the same question."

"Indirectly he already told me," Coach said. "On the drive down, he said he hated to play against you—one of the highest compliments a player can give another player—but he'd love to have you on his team."

"Does he know about you being named the head coach?" I asked.

"You're the only player I've told. Keep it under your hat until it's officially announced."

I nodded. I wasn't sure why he trusted me with this, but I wasn't going to let him down.

• • •

The final buzzer sounded and the Leafs had another moral victory—they'd lost by only two goals, the last one an empty-netter.

"Not a bad game," Coach said. "Especially if you're a Habs fan."

"Cheering for Montreal to win is like getting up at five in the morning and cheering for the sun to rise," I said. "It's gonna happen whether you cheer for it or not."

"He's right," Josh said. "Anybody can be a fan of Montreal. You have to be a real diehard fan to cheer for Toronto."

He held up his hand and we exchanged a high-five.

"I hope neither of you is in a rush to get home," Coach said. "I have a surprise. We're going to meet some people before we leave."

"Who?" I asked.

"If I told you, it wouldn't be a surprise."

We followed him out of the stands and through a corridor. He led us past a pair of security guards—both of whom recognized Coach and shook his hand—and into a sort of party. There were lots of people, sipping on drinks and nibbling on food. Coach was greeted with smiles and handshakes. He seemed to know everybody and everybody seemed to know him. And because they all seemed so glad to see him, they seemed happy to meet us as well.

Some didn't need introductions; they were former Leafs, people I'd either watched on TV or just knew because I knew hockey. The hardest part was mumbling out a few words so I didn't look like a total idiot standing in front of one of my heroes. I fought the urge to ask them for autographs.

What was almost as impressive was watching how the

players treated Coach—with respect. They talked hockey, and while they didn't necessarily agree with everything he said, they certainly didn't argue very hard.

"There's somebody you *really* need to meet," Coach said to us.

We walked toward an older gentleman. He looked familiar . . . then I realized why. He was a former NHL player—a real star in his day. Man, my father would have gone crazy if he'd been there. He gave Coach a smile and the two of them hugged!

"Boys, I'd like you to meet—"

"Terry Fisher," I said, cutting him off. "It's a real honour, sir," I said as we shook hands.

Coach introduced us by name and Mr. Fisher shook Josh's hand as well. Of course, Josh knew of him too, but probably not the way I did.

"Mr. Fisher, you're just about my father's favourite player in the world," I said.

"Call me Terry, son."

"Sure . . . okay. Terry, my father still talks about plays you made."

"Tell your father thanks for me," he said. "My guess is that I've been retired too long for either one of you to have ever seen me play."

"Yes, sir," Josh said.

"Not live, but I've seen footage . . . lots of it," I said. "That goal you scored in game six of the playoffs against Boston in 1985 was unbelievable."

"Lots of people come up and talk to me about that goal, but very few of them are . . . how old are you?"

"I'm turning sixteen, sir."

"Well, not many of them are turning sixteen. It's nice to have people remember." He turned to Coach. "I'm assuming that these two are players."

"*Excellent* players. Both of them will likely be in Junior A this coming year."

"Then I might be seeing more of you two. I'm part of the ownership group of the Watertown Warriors."

"I didn't know that," Josh said.

I didn't know either, but I didn't react, other than to glance over at Coach. He nodded ever so slightly. There was a mischievous look in his eyes, like we were sharing a secret. We *were* sharing a secret.

"It's my hometown, where I live, and where I run my hockey camps," Terry said.

"It must be amazing to own a team," Josh said.

"I'm a *part* owner, and it would be much more amazing if we hadn't finished near the bottom of the standings this year," Terry said. "But I think things are looking up. There are some changes—nothing I can talk about yet—that will help turn things around. Great to meet you boys, and I hope to see more of you."

"Who knows," Josh said, "maybe we'll even be drafted by Watertown."

"We'll just have to keep our fingers crossed," Coach said. He winked at me.

When Terry had left, Coach said, "There's still one more person I want you to meet."

We followed after him, weaving through the crowd.

"There he is!"

I looked over. It was Brad Simmons! He had changed out of his uniform and into a suit that was as fancy as Coach's. I couldn't believe it. Coach called out and Brad waved and walked right toward us. He and Coach shook hands, and then they hugged as well.

"So, Brad, I want you to meet Cody and Josh."

"Nice to meet you, boys," he said.

"That was a good game," Josh said.

"Not for us. I hate losing."

"Especially to Montreal," I added. "I hate Montreal."

"Yes! Exactly!" he exclaimed. "I hate Montreal too!" He put a hand on my shoulder. "Smart kid."

"And a good hockey player," Coach said. "Both of them. Two of the best coming up for the draft this year."

"I remember those days." He nodded his head slowly.

"You boys know that I coached Brad, right?" Coach asked.

"No!" Josh said.

I shook my head. I didn't know either.

"Two years on my team, but also at camps and on tournament teams," Coach said. "He was a *special* player."

Brad looked at his shoes. I would have figured a big star like him would be used to people saying nice things about him. "Thanks, Coach . . . It was good to see you, but I'm sorry, I have to get going."

"Don't be such a stranger in the future. We need to get together for lunch or something," Coach said. "Make sure you don't forget the people who were with you on the way up."

"I won't *ever* forget," he said. "I just gotta go now and meet the guys, like I promised," Brad said. "We're going out for a pop or two."

"Or four or seven," Coach said.

"Could be more."

"Just keep it under control," Coach said. "I can't boss you around anymore, but that doesn't mean I don't still care."

"Sure, thanks. Pleased to meet you, boys. Great to see you, Coach."

He walked back through the crowd, greeting more people as he worked his way across the room and out the door.

"He seems like a terrific guy," Josh said.

"He is," Coach agreed. "Like I said, he's special."

CHAPTER FIVE

Don't screw up," my father said, pushing a finger into my face.

"I'm not going to screw up!" I snapped.

"Are you giving me attitude?"

I knew I'd crossed the line. I could see that flare of anger in his eyes. "No . . . no, sir."

"'Cause it's not like you haven't screwed things up before," he said. "Should we take another look at your last report card?"

I didn't answer. I was passing everything so far, but only barely. And now I was just grateful for a chance to get away—not just from school but from home—and spend some time playing hockey. I wasn't going to let anything get in the way of that . . . not even me.

"You go there and you don't give anybody any attitude or any problems. You understand?"

"Yes, sir."

"You listen to all of the coaches at this camp, but you better be particularly respectful to Coach Connors."

"I will."

They had really got to know Coach through those weekly phone calls. Like always, he'd talk to them before talking to me. He always wanted to know how they were doing and what was new. I think my father saw him as a friend.

"Just remember, he's the man who arranged all of this. And he's not just one of the coaches at this camp. Now, with his new position . . . who knows?" my father said.

There was no need to say anything else. The road to the NHL ran right through Junior A, and the draft was the invitation to get on that road—the key to the kingdom. Showing what I could do at this camp was the first step to getting noticed by the Junior A scouts, and Coach was helping me take it.

"And I'm telling you right now, if you cause trouble and get tossed out, you better find someplace else to stay because you're sure as hell not coming back here!"

"He'll do fine," my mother said.

"Are you arguing with me now?" he demanded.

"No, of course not," she mumbled.

She looked like she was trying to make herself small.

She didn't have to be afraid of him. If he even dared to put a hand on her . . . well . . . no more.

"He better do more than just fine. It's not like he's going to make it on his brains or looks," my father said. "This is the ticket to our . . . I mean, *his* dreams."

"I understand, and I'm going to do great," I said. He was an idiot, but he was right about this. This was my shot. I was going to this camp to not only increase my skills but to increase my visibility. I was going to be *seen*. Coach Connors had made me understand just how connected the hockey community was. Everybody knew everybody else, and a good word or a bad reputation spread fast.

My mother reached over and gave me a hug. "I'll miss you," she whispered in my ear.

"Me too."

I slung my hockey bag over my shoulder, then picked up my suitcase with one hand and grabbed my two sticks with the other. I was ready. At least, as ready as I could be.

• • •

"Come on, pick it up, pick it up!" one of the coaches yelled.

My lungs were burning, but I dug deeper, going faster. I didn't care if I coughed up a lung; I wasn't giving in to the pain. I just blocked it out. I was already in the lead in laps, but I wasn't going to let anybody get any closer to me. Making them look bad made me look better. I wasn't as skilled as some of these guys, and I certainly didn't have the fancy equipment most of them had arrived with, but *nobody* was going to outwork me.

I put my head down and pumped harder and harder. A coach blew his whistle and everybody around me started to glide. I didn't. I took a half-dozen more strides, still digging, so that nobody would have any question about who had won.

"Five minutes . . . five minutes . . . get some water!" he yelled.

I needed water. Dehydration was always a danger. If you didn't take in enough water, you could cramp up. I grabbed my bottle from the bench.

"Looking good out there," Coach Connors said.

"Trying," I huffed as I gulped down a drink.

"Succeeding. You're working hard. People are noticing. *I've* noticed."

"Thanks."

"You been thinking much about the draft?" he asked.

"Yep."

"You should be. Are you still feeling okay about leaving home if you're drafted by a team that's in the sticks?"

"Like your team?" I asked.

"Like my team."

"I meant it when I said I'm ready to go wherever I have the best shot at making it."

He nodded knowingly.

I'd go anywhere. I didn't have a steady girlfriend or any

really close friends, and going to a new school could only be a change for the better, and my parents . . . well . . . I'd miss my mother.

Coach crooked a finger toward me and skated away from the other players. I followed.

"Would you mind me asking you a question?" he asked.

"Sure . . . of course."

"I know that players get really attached to their equipment . . . like your gloves . . . you've had those for a long time, right?"

"A long time." It wasn't that I was attached to them or that they were that comfortable, but a pair of gloves—heck, all the equipment—was expensive. I couldn't afford new ones.

"Would you consider wearing new gloves and maybe some new shoulder pads?" he said, tapping my pads.

"Yeah, I guess." All I needed was the money.

"Great!" he said, and he slapped me on the back. "I'll bring them to you tomorrow."

"But I don't have the money . . . you know . . . here with me."

"No, no, you wouldn't have to pay for them. They were given to me by the manufacturer. It will actually help them, be good promotion, to have a player like you wearing their equipment."

"Really?"

"Don't be so surprised. Things change at the next

level. You'll find out," he said. "I can bring them along tomorrow." He paused. "But that might not be such a wise thing."

He looked around to see if anyone was watching or listening. He moved in a little closer. "I just don't want the other players to see me giving them to you in case they think I'm giving you special favours—even if I am."

"Oh, right. What if I picked them up?"

"No," he said, shaking his head. "Probably too risky."

"What would be risky?"

"You'd have to, you know, slip out of the residence. What if someone asks where you're going?"

"I don't have to tell anybody anything. And I could be back before curfew."

"That would be great. It's just that with the draft coming up, I don't want to tip my hand to anybody about players I'm interested in. That I've got my eye on you, that's between me and you . . . and, of course, Terry," he said, gesturing to Coach Fisher. "I've told him I'd like to see you on our team. Of course, he has the final say on these things."

"And what does he think?"

"Just keep on doing what you're doing to impress him."

A whistle sounded and Terry called for everybody to come toward centre.

"Here's my address," Coach Connors said, and he slipped me a piece of paper.

I tucked the paper into my glove and snugged it into one of the fingers.

"See you around eight. That'll give you enough time to get back before curfew."

"Thanks."

I joined the coaches. I wasn't the first to get there, but I certainly wasn't the last. Some people were still getting up. Tired legs weren't keeping them up or pushing them along very fast.

Terry stood at the centre of the circle. This was his camp and *technically* he was the head coach, but it was clear to everybody else that he was probably the worst of the four coaches on his staff. The best was also pretty clear. Coach Connors was head and shoulders above everybody else.

The reason the camp was in Watertown, the reason Terry had bought into the Watertown team, was that he'd grown up and still lived right there. His name was even on the signs when you came into town—"Welcome to Watertown, Home of Terry Fisher." He was the most famous person who had ever come out of the place.

I had to admit that he seemed like a good guy, but in some ways he reminded me of my father. They didn't look alike, and I hadn't even seen Terry take a drink, but it was like he was some old guy, telling his hockey stories and coasting along on past glories. My father was the same. The biggest difference, I guess, was that at least Terry had some real glories to talk about.

Coach Connors had explained to me that he'd been a coach in the camp the last five years, and when the head coaching spot on the Warriors had opened up, it was Terry himself who had decided to hire him. I figured I should be grateful to Terry for that, at least.

"Well, men," Terry began, "we're almost at the end of day two."

He always called us "men," although that was stretching it for some of the guys there. He started talking and I drifted off. It didn't matter whether it was on the ice or in a class, I didn't have much time for being talked at. He really *did* remind me of my father.

Coach Connors stood right beside Terry, and it was obvious which one of the two had been in the NHL. Terry was a good four inches taller, and the only place Coach Connors was thicker than him was in the gut. Even though Terry was older and had been retired for a long time, he still looked like a player—thick neck, muscular arms, wide in the back and shoulders. In the day, he'd been known for his toughness—crushing checks and digging in the corners. He could still out-skate all the other coaches and most of the players. I wouldn't have wanted to go into a corner with Terry for a puck. Although if I did, I could guarantee that he'd have to hurt me to stop me.

As Terry continued to talk, I looked at Coach Connors. He really didn't look much like a hockey player— which he wasn't. He'd never played at any level above house league. He was big, but he had more in common with the guy in the bleachers who was selling beer and popcorn. He wasn't exactly fat, but the word *pudgy* certainly would have fit. Still, if you were just watching him and Terry, you'd have guessed wrong about which one knew his hockey stuff the best.

Coach Fisher was always yelling about "digging deeper" and "going the distance," but he really didn't know much about teaching. Coach Connors had very specific drills and exercises designed to make you a better player. He *was* making me a better player, the way he was making everybody in camp better. If he'd been my coach for the season, we would have done a lot better—maybe even won it all . . . something Coach Connors had done at every level he'd ever coached. It would be *amazing* to have him as my coach and . . . I put a stop to my thoughts. What if I was drafted by another team before he had a shot? What if I wasn't drafted at all? There was no point in getting too high. It only made the fall harder. I knew better, really. Wishing for something was a guarantee it wouldn't come true. Wishes were never granted and prayers were never answered. That's why I'd given up on both of them. Hard work was the only thing that had a chance.

"Okay, men, that's it," Terry said. "Hit the showers and let's call it a day!"

There were hoots from the crowd and a rush to the gate leading off the ice to the dressing room and the showers. I was in no hurry to leave and I didn't really understand why the rest of the guys were. They'd paid a lot of money—well, most of them—to attend an expensive hockey camp, and all they wanted to do now was get *off* the ice. As they headed for the gate, I skated down to the far end of the rink. There was a net and dozens of pucks scattered around. I'd stay until somebody kicked me off.

The arena got quieter and quieter as the ice emptied. Sometimes I thought the only thing better than the roar of a crowd was the silence of a completely empty arena.

I pushed one of the pucks forward, stickhandling, keeping it at the centre of the stick, right in the sweet spot on the blade. Back and forth, back and forth. The only way to get better was to practise. I figured that each second on the ice was like dropping a few pennies in a piggy bank. They added up, and then when you needed them in a game, you could make a withdrawal. Pushing yourself, making your lungs and legs log more time when they wanted to rest, was what you drew on in the game. Everybody who wasn't stupid knew what to do, but most didn't have enough gas in the tank to make it happen. They'd see the puck in the corner but couldn't get it. They'd try to shove somebody off the puck but wouldn't have the strength. They'd know where to shoot the puck, but their muscles couldn't make it happen.

Next I drew the puck in and then out, playing with it like it was on a string, offering it to the imaginary defender and drawing it back just as he tried to take it. I did a fake around that defender and snapped my shot, high and so tight that it clinked against the post before being caught by the netting. I felt a little rush of adrenalin—as always.

I circled out to the blue line. There were ten or twelve pucks scattered out there. One by one, I lined them up side by side, and then I shot each puck. I took a couple of snap shots, a wrist shot, and four or five slapshots. Half of them connected and the others sailed high and wide. That was okay; the secret wasn't to hit the centre of the net but to pick the corners. Any idiot could hit the goalie, but that wasn't how you scored goals.

I skated toward the net and a puck flew past me and into the mesh—top-right corner. I turned around. It was Coach Fisher—Terry.

"Nice shot," I noted.

"You took a few good ones yourself. You're two for two," he said.

I didn't know what that meant—I'd taken dozens of shots already.

"Two days of camp and both days you've been the last one off the ice. You're a real rink rat."

"You have to take your ice time when you can get it."

"You're right about that. Back in the day, it was free. We'd just go down to the pond and play shinny until either it got too dark or our feet froze off."

Great. Another story about "the day."

"There are no ponds where I come from."

"Probably just rinks and rules and refs and teams.

Pond shinny is where you get your grit from . . . not that you're doing too shabby in that department," he said.

I knew what a compliment that was coming from him.

"They're going to kick us both off soon so they can resurface the ice. Put the pucks into the net and we'll gather them from there," he said.

We started shooting or tapping the pucks into the net. He shot them hard, still putting them in the corners. I did the same and quickly realized that we were in an unspoken contest. I'd shoot one into the bottom-left corner and he'd do the same with his next shot. If I went top shelf, then he went top shelf.

"I figure your dream is to make the Show, right?" he asked as he hit the net again.

"Isn't that everybody's dream?"

"Yeah, everybody I grew up with," he agreed. "Of course, most don't make it. Sixty kids in this camp and no more than six have a shot at it."

"I was thinking it was less than that."

He chuckled. "I said a shot. Not making it. And do you think you're one of them?"

"Doesn't matter what I think," I replied. I snapped another shot, low, more centre than I would have liked— an easy stop for any goalie. "What's more important is, what do *you* think?"

"I *think* there are players in this camp who are more skilled than you, and I *know* there are players who are bigger than you."

"I heard that the bigger they are, the harder they fall."

"Usually the harder they fall right on top of you," he said, and laughed.

"So am I one of those six?" I asked.

"I guess we'll have to wait and see," he said.

Well, maybe he didn't believe in me, but I knew somebody who *did*.

"Making it is about more than skill or size," he said.

The big gates at the end opened and the Zamboni was there, running, waiting to come on.

"We better clear off," he said. "But there's still one puck left." He pointed into the far corner.

"I'll get it."

"We'll see about that!" he exclaimed.

He put a hand on my shoulder and yanked me back as he started racing toward the corner. I jumped forward and chased. He was going to beat me there . . . but that was no guarantee of who would come out of the corner with the puck!

CHAPTER SIX

Hey, Cody, we're heading downtown to get some pizza," Tanner said. "You want to join us?"

"First off, Watertown doesn't have anything that could be called downtown, and second, I'm thinking no."

Funny, I thought, if Coach Connors did draft me, this place would be my home for the next three or four years. Watertown wasn't very big—it was nothing like living in Toronto—but I would have killed to call this place home. It would mean not just being in the OHL but having a great coach, somebody who believed in me, to help me make it to the next level, the ultimate level. I stopped myself again. No point in dreaming too much or too big. Not yet.

"Come on, it'll be fun," said Colby, another one of my bunk mates. "You just gonna hang around here instead?"

"No, I'm going to head out. I got someplace to go." Now I'd have to come up with a lie, fast, to explain where I was going and what I was going to be—

"Does she at least have a friend?" Tanner asked.

I smiled. So much for *me* having to come up with a lie.

"I'm sure she has lots of friends," I said. "I just don't know if any of them are desperate enough to want to be with you."

"How about with me?" Colby asked.

"For you we'd have to find somebody who was desperate *and* blind."

"And don't forget me," Ben added as he came out of the bathroom, wearing just a towel.

"Look, men—and believe me, I'm just using that term to be polite—I understand how you three probably *need* somebody to get women for you, but isn't it enough that I carry your sorry butts around the ice? Do I really need to get you women as well?"

"*Need* is a pretty strong word," Colby said. "We don't need women."

"Speak for yourself!" Ben said and gave him a push.

Colby grabbed Ben and the two started to wrestle.

"I told you he didn't need women!" Ben screamed as his towel flopped off and he and Colby rolled around on the carpet. "He's after my privates! Help, help, he's trying to do me!"

Colby pushed him away and jumped to his feet while Ben grabbed his towel and wrapped it around himself again.

"Come on, Cody," Tanner said. "She doesn't have to have three friends, just one—okay, maybe two—for me."

"You couldn't handle two women!" Ben laughed.

"Shut up or I'll shove you out the door and into the hall with just your towel . . . or with *no* towel," Tanner said.

Ben looked worried. "I don't know if Colby could control himself if he saw me naked again." He pulled his towel a bit tighter around his waist. "So, are you going to get us some women?"

"Why don't you just get your own puck-bunnies?" I suggested. "There have to be girls with low standards in this town."

"There must be at least *one*," Ben said. "After all, *you* have a date."

In one move, I grabbed Ben and spun him around so that his arms were pinned behind him.

"Open the door!" I yelled.

"No, you can't—!"

Tanner opened the door and I pushed Ben toward the opening. Just as he was about to exit, Colby grabbed the towel away and I shoved the naked Ben out the door and into the hall. I released his arms and he just got his hands up before he smacked into the wall on the other side of the hallway! I slammed the door closed.

Ben threw himself against the door. "Come on, let me in!" he hollered and started pounding against it.

I put on the chain lock and opened the door just the little distance it would go.

"Let me in!" he screamed.

"You should try to keep it down so you don't attract attention," I suggested. I turned to Colby and took the towel. "Here," I said as I offered it to Ben. He tried to take it, but I snatched it back inside and out of his reach. "You don't look grateful. Shouldn't you at least say thank you for my generous offer?"

He looked too stunned, embarrassed, and angry to even think of what to reply.

"Because if the local girls get a look at your, shall we say, merchandise, the only puck-bunnies you're going to get will have short expectations or little dreams."

Tanner and Colby were cracking up behind me.

"Give me my towel!" he yelled.

"So what's the magic word?" I asked.

Ben looked mad enough to spit.

"Well?"

"Could I *please* have my towel?" he asked.

"I'm *hearing* the word, but I'm just not *feeling* it."

"Cody, don't—"

He stopped as we both heard voices coming down the hall.

"Too late to apologize," I said, and I slammed the door closed.

He started pounding on the door again. I clicked off the chain, opened it, and he fell into the room, landing on the floor!

"Here's your towel," I said, and we all exploded into laughter.

He scrambled for it, covering up and jumping to his feet.

This was the moment. Either he was going to take a swing at me or—he burst into a big smile. "You pervert."

"Me? It wasn't me who was butt-naked in the hall, flashing people as they went by. You're the perv!"

I opened the door. "Do you know where you're going for that pizza?"

"Dominic's is the name of it, I think," Tanner said.

"We'll see what happens. Maybe I'll show up with her and some of her friends."

"That would be fantastic!" Colby said.

"Yeah, amazing," Ben agreed.

"But no promises. If I'm choosing between a piece of pizza and a *piece*, you know which one I'm gonna take!"

They all laughed and gave me high-fives and slaps on the back. This was all so convincing that I had to remind myself that I wasn't really going to see some girl. That would have been good, but new gloves and shoulder pads were even better. I started thinking that the ideal girl would have a father who owned a sporting goods store and a pizza place.

I bent down and picked up my sports bag.

"What's in the bag?" Tanner asked.

At that moment, the answer was "Nothing"—I was just bringing it to put my new stuff in—but I couldn't say that.

"You never know what you might need. A guy has to be like a boy scout . . . prepared for anything."

They all hooted.

"So if I'm not here at curfew, could you three cover for me?" I asked.

"Who says *we're* going to be here?" Ben asked.

"Why, are you going to order a second pizza?"

More laughter. I figured he was smart enough not to chirp at me anymore.

"I guess we'll see," I said. "Don't wait up."

I left, closing the door behind me. The only issue was that I couldn't show up back at the residence before them, or until just before curfew, or they'd figure that my date had gone bad. I chuckled. I now had to make a fake date appear successful. That could be a problem. It wasn't like it was going to take me long to pick up the equipment, and I couldn't wander around downtown without the risk of being seen by them. I'd just have to make up some story about her father coming home early, or how she was a churchy girl and I knew I was wasting my time. I had always been able to come up with a lie pretty fast to cover up for something that I'd done wrong. My father wasn't into forgiveness or understanding, so I'd learned that a lie was often easier than the truth—and a lot less painful.

Passing through the common room on my way out the door, I had to walk through about thirty guys who were all focused on the big-screen TV and the Xbox NHL game going on. Four players were working the controls while everybody else was cheering them on like it was a real game. They were all yelling and laughing and screaming to be heard over the loud music they had playing.

For most of them, this was as close as they were ever going to get to the NHL unless they bought a ticket. Video games were such a waste of time. If some of these guys had spent nearly as much time working on their wrist shots as twisting their wrists around to work the controller, they might actually have had a shot at the real thing.

I didn't own an Xbox, so there wasn't any big temptation for me to play, but even if I'd had one, I wouldn't have played it . . . more than occasionally. I wasted enough time going to school, so there was no way I was going to waste any more on stupid video games. Ice time might have been expensive and hard to get, but a couple of pieces of plywood—one on the ground as the ice and the other on the wall as the net—were dirt cheap. I couldn't even guess how much time I'd spent in the basement or on the driveway shooting. I guess the only real clues were the dents in the garage door and the marks on the basement wall . . . and a couple that dinged the dryer as well.

The secret to anything—whether it was hockey, hockey video games, or, I guess, playing the violin—was to just practise. I'd long ago figured out which of those was the best use of my time, but I also knew that if I *did* decide to play the violin, I'd learn how to play it well. I wouldn't be wasting my time playing violin video games . . . was there even such a thing? Probably not, because who wanted to even play the *real* violin to begin with?

I slipped around the mob as they watched the game unfold. I opened the door and exited, nobody having seen me leave.

CHAPTER SEVEN

I looked up at the building and down at the piece of paper Coach Connors had given me. This was the right place. It just wasn't what I'd expected. This dump didn't match either his fancy car or his expensive suits.

I pushed open the door and there was a strange odour . . . stale . . . sour . . . it smelled *poor*. I knew that smell. I went into the stairwell and another aroma was added— urine. Up two flights to the top floor and then down the hall, looking for 311. I stopped at the door and listened. Music was coming through the door. It was faint but familiar. I listened harder and recognized the voice. It was one of my father's favourites, The Rolling Stones.

I knocked on the door, and within seconds it opened up and the music got louder.

"Hey, Cody!" Coach Connors exclaimed. "Good to see you! Come on in!"

I walked into the apartment. The furniture wasn't much better than the rest of the building. And strangely, the curtains were not just pulled shut but held shut with duct tape—why would he do that?

"Hang on!" he yelled over the music. He walked over to an iPod dock and turned down the volume. "I guess that isn't the kind of thing you listen to."

"Not really, but my father loves The Stones and Led Zeppelin and all that classic rock stuff."

"Classic rock rules!" he said with a laugh. "They are never going to make music like that again. Mick and Keith strutted the stage like nobody else ever did or ever will."

I shrugged. Whatever. Anyway, liking something my father liked wasn't impressive.

"You have to think of them as being to music what guys like Gretzky, Messier, and Coffey—or before that Howe, Lindsay, and Abel—were to hockey. The Stones weren't just about music but about attitude. They *knew* who they were."

"Okay . . ."

"So, do you want something to drink?" he asked.

"Sure, that would be great."

He picked up a glass. "I'm drinking wine myself. Would you like some wine, or maybe a beer?"

"A beer?"

He laughed. "Don't act like you've never had one before."

"Of course I've had a beer."

"I could get you a soft drink instead, if you really want one."

"No, I'll take the beer," I said.

"Good. I mean, what's the point of pretending? And anyway, I think it's artificial to assign an age when somebody is old enough to have a drink. I know some sixteen-year-olds who are mature enough to drink and some sixty-year-olds who shouldn't be allowed anything stronger than fruit punch, you know what I mean? So, I have Blue, Canadian, Coors Light . . . what do you want?"

"Canadian would be fine."

"Is that what your father drinks?" he asked.

"My father drinks whatever's put in front of him."

I sat down on a couch. Coach went into the kitchen and I could see through the doorway as he opened up the fridge. There wasn't much food in there, but there was a lot of beer. Funny, he'd never struck me as much of a drinker—maybe he had more in common with my father than his taste in music.

He walked back in and handed me the beer, and I twisted off the cap.

"Cheers," he said, and he clinked his glass against the bottle.

"Cheers."

I hesitated. I felt a little uneasy. Was this a test or something?

"Drink up," he said.

If it was a test, I'd already failed, so what else could I do? I took a sip of the beer.

"Probably better to keep this just between us," he said. "Or maybe just tell your old man . . . he'd understand."

Again, not much question there. He *would* understand having a drink, but I'd learned not to tell him anything.

"I don't know anybody who didn't have a beer or two before they were legal age. I just think it's better that it's done under supervision instead of in some alley or in a park," Coach said.

That did make sense.

"Not much of a place," he said, looking a bit embarrassed as he glanced around the apartment. He settled into a chair that sat directly across from a big-screen TV—for sure the most expensive thing there. "I just rented it when Terry appointed me coach. To be honest, I don't plan on spending much time here anyway. I practically live at the arena during the season."

"What's up with the windows?" I asked, gesturing to the curtains, which were duct-taped shut.

"Sometimes I sleep at strange times and I like it dark. Besides, I don't like people peeking in, snooping into my life. I like my privacy . . . which is hard when you live in the public eye. Especially in a place as small as Watertown." He paused. "So, what do you think of the camp so far?"

"It's good. I'm enjoying it . . . learning a lot."

"I watched you go into the corner with Terry after

practice today," he said. "Pretty cool to be going up against a former big-leaguer."

I smiled. It was pretty cool.

"He's still as strong as an ox," Coach Connors said.

"Tell me about it. I gave him a shoulder and he just shrugged me off."

"Man against boy. You'll grow and develop, build some more muscle. Who knows where you might end up ... someday ..."

He let the sentence trail off, but we both knew what he meant—maybe someday I could be in the Show too.

"Terry's a solid guy," Coach Connors said. "This is the fifth year I've worked with him at the camps, and now, being his next head coach, it's even better. He's always straightforward, no problems, no hassles. He's a pillar of this community ... so respected. He and I are *tight*," he said, holding up two fingers side by side. "Like I already told you, who you know counts for a lot in this business."

"But you're a great coach. Isn't that enough?"

"I *am* a great coach, but it's connections that get you where you need to go. Remember that. My connection to Terry opened the door ... maybe for both of us."

"I guess he's a good guy," I said.

"He is. Not much of a coach, mind you, but a good guy." He paused. "I guess I shouldn't have said that. You might think he's a great coach."

I shook my head. "I know who's really running the school." I pointed at him, and he smiled.

"Thanks for noticing. You're a smart kid."

"You want to tell that to my teachers?" I asked.

"Oh, don't worry about it too much. Some people are smart in school and stupid in life and on the ice. I know you had problems in school this year," he said. "Your father told me all about it . . . a few times."

"I'm passing," I said defensively.

"I know, but the suspensions could have been avoided."

I'd had three suspensions—one for cutting classes, one for being "disrespectful" to a teacher who didn't deserve respect, and another for a fight. The last one I didn't regret at all.

"The problem is that people see you having trouble in school and they think that means you'll be trouble on their team," he said.

"I've never been trouble for a team!" I protested.

"I know that. But it's like having low marks and people not understanding that there are different types of smart. To some people, trouble is just trouble." He finished off the wine in his glass and poured himself another. "So, tell me, what do you think about the other players in our camp?" he asked.

I wasn't sure what to say. I had opinions, but was it really okay for me to share them?

"Don't be shy; I'm not just asking for fun. I want to know more about your hockey IQ. I want to know if you *really* know hockey."

I still wasn't sure how honest I ought to be.

"Look, I'm not going to tell anybody what you think, and I know that you won't tell them what I think about Terry. I trust *you*, and you have to learn to trust *me*. Okay?"

I nodded. "Well . . . there are some guys who really know what they're doing," I said. "You have some *players*."

"And some who aren't?"

I laughed. "Lots. There are *players* and there are *posers*," I said. "Some people are only here because their parents have the money."

"No argument from me there. The way I see it, there are really only three players that have any chance of moving up. A couple more may have the skills, but they don't have the heart. If you don't have the passion, the desire to learn, and a willingness to listen to the coach, then having the skills means nothing."

I nodded again.

"I want you to look at these." He pulled out a binder from underneath the coffee table and placed it in front of me, opening it up to reveal a picture of one of the guys in the camp. "There's a section on every player," he said. "A few pictures, and then extensive notes about them."

That explained why he'd been taking pictures while we were on the ice.

"In a hockey camp my goals are realistic. I just want to make everybody better. And for me to help them, I really have to know them. I look at strengths, weaknesses, tendencies. I can't help them become better players until I know what they need to work on."

"That makes sense," I agreed.

"Have a look at the book and let me know what you think. I'll get you another beer."

"I'm not finished this one," I said, holding it up.

"Well, when you're ready, there's plenty more where that came from . . . unless you can't handle your alcohol?"

"I can handle it." I tipped the bottle back and chugged it down, a little escaping from my mouth and dripping down my chin as the rest went down my throat.

He went to the kitchen while I drained the dregs in my bottle. When he came back, he had another Canadian for me.

"By the way," he said, "you should read the section on you."

• • •

I closed the book on the final player and took a slug from my fourth beer.

"So, what do you think?" he asked.

"I agree with what you wrote . . . you just wrote so much."

"Some coaches think that scouting is just about watching what a player does on the ice, but I know better. You really have to get to know the guy, who he is, his family background, what makes him tick."

"And what you wrote about me . . . do you really think I could make it . . . ?" I let the sentence trail off.

"I believe you have the potential. If you have the right coaching, you have a shot at the big time. Like I said at the rink, I believe in you enough to risk a draft pick on you this summer."

"Really?"

"If you're still available at the right place in the draft, then I'm going to pull the trigger. But you have to understand that I'm not going to take you with my first or second pick."

"You're not?"

"Don't be disappointed," he said.

He was even better at reading my feelings than I was at hiding them, and I'd spent years learning to bury them deep.

"The draft is just a big game. I have to make guesses, educated guesses, about where players will go, what value other scouts have assigned them, and I have to risk that you won't be taken until later. It's not that other coaches don't think you have the skills. They just wonder if the problems in school and with your family make you a risk. You have to understand that none of that is a secret. Like I said, everybody is connected one way or another."

"I understand . . . it's just that school isn't the rink, and it's not fair to blame me if my father gets mouthy at the arena!"

"I know that," he said. "Part of being a good scout and a good coach is that you have to learn about the person. And I like what I see."

"Thanks." It was a relief to hear that he believed in me. I didn't get that from many people.

"There are lots of coaches, but not a lot of *good* coaches," he said.

"And you're a good coach." I laughed. "Although this is the first time I've ever shared a beer with one of my coaches."

"Well, you're not a kid anymore—I can see that every time you're on the ice—so drink up. You've earned it!" He knocked back the wine in his own glass—I always thought wine was for sipping, but maybe not.

"Part of being a coach," he said, picking up the subject again, "is knowing the players I coach *against*. You have to know how to exploit weaknesses, look for bad habits, patterns. Good scouting and good coaching work together to win games. I think I showed that again this year."

"For sure . . . congratulations on winning the division again," I said.

"Three years in a row. That's what gave me the chance to move up a level—well, that and knowing Terry. Never forget the personal connections."

"Do you ever think about coaching at the next level, in the NHL?"

"Who wouldn't? But I really think my strength is with younger players. Coaching them, helping them to develop—that's where my passion is," he explained. "You never know, though, what will happen in the future. Life is full of surprises. But for now I'm going to work with those players who are willing to make the sacrifices." He lifted his glass in a toast. We clinked again, and then I gulped some more down.

"So, does anybody know you're here this evening?" he asked.

"Nobody. Hardly anybody even knows that I'm out."

"Hardly anybody?"

"My roommates know I was heading out, but they don't know where," I explained.

"And they weren't curious?"

"I told them I was going out to see some girl in town."

He laughed. "Very smart, and very believable. You are obviously a very good liar."

I wasn't sure what to say to that.

He laughed again. "Don't worry. That's all right. When I'm coaching, there are lots of things I don't say. Some things don't need to be talked about, or shouldn't be talked about."

Okay, that was better.

"Come here, I want to show you something," he said.

I got up—I felt a little buzzed. The beer, especially drunk that fast, had gone to my head and my legs. He led me out of the room and into the bedroom. Taped to the wall were a bunch of big white bristol boards, and on them were pictures of hockey players and newspaper and magazine stories about them.

"This is my wall of fame. Do you know what all of these players have in common?" he asked.

I looked, studying, trying to figure out the answer to his question. I knew some of them—they were NHL players—but there were others in minor league uniforms who I didn't know.

Unable to come up with the answer, I shook my head.

"I've coached *all* of those players," he said proudly. "Either while they were on my team or at a camp. *All* of them. I had a hand in them getting to where they are now."

"That's amazing. I didn't know you coached him," I said, pointing to one of my favourite NHL players.

"He's a good guy. Next time he's in town, maybe I can arrange for you to meet him."

"Are you serious?"

"Of course I'm serious. He remembers where he came from and who helped him along the way. But do you know what's the most amazing thing about this wall?" he asked.

I shook my head.

He pointed to a big blank spot in the middle of the display. "I always leave that spot open because there's still room for somebody else to make it." He looked at me. "Somebody like you."

I didn't even know what to say.

"It could happen, and it all starts now, tonight, right now. Do you believe it's possible?" he asked.

"I'll do everything, *anything*, I need to do to make it happen," I replied.

"I'm counting on that," he said. He gave me a big

slap on the shoulder. "Now, let's get you those gloves and shoulder pads."

He opened up a closet. There were a few suits hanging there, but mostly it was filled with sticks and gloves, a set of goalie pads, helmets, and other equipment. He pulled out a pair of gloves and looked at them. "Try them on."

I slipped them on.

"Well?"

"They feel good."

"Leave one on, and then slip on one of these and tell me which feels better."

He handed me a right glove from a second pair, and I slipped off the right one I was wearing and handed it to him.

"Hold the stick," he said, handing one to me. "Which one feels right?"

I gripped the stick, flexing my fingers. Both gloves were good, but one was better. "This one," I said, holding it up.

"Nice choice." He handed me the left glove from that pair.

"Now take off your shirt," he said.

"What?"

"So you can try on the shoulder pads," he explained.

"Oh ... sure," I mumbled. I felt awkward. Even though I was used to changing in front of other players in the dressing room, this was no dressing room.

He pulled out a pair of pads from the closet. "They look about the right size."

He handed them to me and I took off my shirt and slipped them on. I started to adjust them and he helped, tightening the straps, snugging them into place.

"They look like a good fit," he said. "How do they feel?"

"Nice. Expensive."

"They *are* expensive, but you need to have the right equipment. If you'd been wearing these pads today, you wouldn't have a sore shoulder right now," he said.

"How do you know I have a sore shoulder?"

He laughed. "I know everything."

"Seriously."

He laughed again. "I saw your reaction after you blocked that shot in the scrimmage. It caught you under the padding . . . right here."

He pushed his finger into my shoulder and I grimaced in pain.

"Sorry, didn't mean to hurt you, just wanted to show you. The problem is that because of the pain, you started to protect your shoulder and it affected your shot. You know that breakaway you missed?"

"How could I forget?"

"You missed because you didn't have full mobility when you went to your backhand after the deke. In the Show, they'd have a physiotherapist, a chiropractor, an exercise physiologist, and a massage therapist who would be working with you right away . . . maybe even in the intermission."

"That's amazing."

"Next year I'm going to arrange for a massage therapist to help my team. Have you ever had a massage?" he
asked.

"Never."

"It's very therapeutic. Sit down," he said, gesturing to
the bed, "and take off the shoulder pads."

The whole idea of getting a massage from anyone, let
alone a guy, made me a little uncomfortable, but I did
what he said.

"I'm no massage therapist, but I know some of the
techniques. Turn around."

From behind me he placed his hands on my shoulders. "Man, are you tense. You're as hard as a rock."

I was feeling pretty tense and really sore.

"Massage can have lots of uses. It can help with tired
muscles. It can help repair strains. It can feel good or it
can actually hurt. How does this feel?"

"Um . . . okay . . . fine, I guess."

"You've got a bad knot," he said. "Deep-tissue massage
can free up muscles like that."

He dug his fingers into my back, just under the shoulder blades, and I had to fight to not jump up and yell at
him to stop.

"Sometimes it can be a little painful," he said. He
released the pressure. "I know that hurt, but how does it
feel now?"

I shrugged the shoulder and then rotated it. "It feels
better, a *lot* better."

"Oh, hey, you should get going," Coach said. He pointed at a clock on the dresser.

"It's almost curfew!" I exclaimed.

I jumped to my feet and grabbed my shirt, the shoulder pads, and the gloves from the floor and hurried back into the living room. I slid my arms into the sleeves of my shirt and then stuffed the equipment in the bag that I'd brought with me. Quickly I grabbed my coat and put it on.

"I lost track of the time!"

"We both did," he said. "You'd better rush."

"I will, and thanks for the gloves and the pads. I really appreciate it."

"It's my pleasure. Just tell people you had them in your suitcase if anybody asks," he said.

"I will."

"And remember, there are always a couple of beers here in the fridge waiting for you."

"Thanks. Good night."

After he closed the door, I took a few steps down the dimly lit hall and then just stopped. I took a deep breath. Here I was, new equipment in the bag, having just been told that I had what it was going to take, that he believed in me, that I was going to be drafted in Junior A. I should have felt like I was walking on air, but instead I felt just . . . just . . . off.

Then my stomach lurched and I realized I was on the verge of throwing up. I tried to keep it down and stumbled into the stairwell where I promptly threw up all over the stairs. The vomit—clear and liquidy, smelling of the beer that made up most of it—washed down the stairs, dripping from stair to stair. Well, at least it wouldn't smell like piss anymore.

Carefully, a hand on the railing to steady myself, I walked down the stairs, stepping around the mess I'd made.

CHAPTER EIGHT

The cold, clean air felt good in my lungs, although my legs still felt a little bit wobbly. I'd thrown up a second time on the street, probably from trying to move too fast. I slowed down. I was already five minutes late for my eleven o'clock curfew and there was no rolling back time . . . wait, didn't Superman do that once in a comic? He flew really fast, circling the world, and he slowed it down and made it turn backwards. Who said I couldn't read and absorb stuff? If I could have done my book reports on comics or graphic novels, my marks would have soared. I just didn't have the time to waste on a novel.

The residence was just up ahead. I crossed the road and then the grass so I was walking right up against the wall of the building, hidden in the shadows. I came up to the door and peeked through the window. There were a dozen guys sitting in the common area, still playing Xbox. I drew back my head so I wouldn't be seen. It was after curfew, but it wouldn't be lights out for another forty-five minutes. If I walked in now, the odds were that somebody was going to notice. Maybe it would be better if I just waited until everybody went to their rooms, and then I could sneak in—assuming they didn't lock the doors. I couldn't take that chance.

Quietly, slowly, I opened the door. Nobody turned away from the game. I was in the clear.

"Curfew is at eleven, Cody." Coach Terry.

"Sorry, sir, I lost track of time."

He leaned in closer and took a deep sniff. "Did you lose track of our non-drinking policy too?"

He gestured for me to follow him down the hallway to the office. I saw that nobody had noticed any of this. I was at least grateful for that. He closed the door behind us and sat down behind his desk while I took the chair in front.

"So, tell me what happened," he said. "You smell like you've been drinking."

"Um . . . a guy spilled a drink on me."

"It smells like he spilled it down your throat," he said. "A number of times. Look, Cody, you can't con a con, and you can't fool an alcoholic."

What was that supposed to mean?

"I'm an alcoholic," he said. "I've been dry for almost ten years, but I'm still an alcoholic."

"But doesn't that make you an ex-alcoholic?" I asked.

"Once an alcoholic, always an alcoholic," he said, correcting me.

"Oh yeah, that's right. I remember them saying that at the meeting," I said.

"You've been to a meeting about alcoholism?"

"I was forced to go to a couple of those Alateen things."

He nodded his head knowingly. "It's good that teenagers have support groups like that. Can I ask? Is it your father, or your mother, or someone else in your life?"

"My father. My mother doesn't drink at all."

"Your father has a drinking problem," he said.

"He doesn't think so. As long as he has enough to drink, he doesn't figure he has any problem at all," I said, trying to joke around. Just then I wished that I were a lot more sober, because the way my head was still swimming, I had a feeling I might say just about anything, and that wasn't too smart.

"It's still probably a problem for all those around him. If you'd like, I could talk to him," he said.

"No!" I exclaimed, surprising myself with the force of my answer. "I mean, no, thank you, sir . . . it's okay."

"I wouldn't talk to him without your permission. But if now's not the right time . . . often people have to hit bottom before they look for help."

I didn't know how much further my father could sink. It was scary to think that he hadn't reached bottom yet.

"You should keep going to those meetings," Terry said.

"Why? I'm not the one with a drinking problem."

Coach Terry got up and circled around till he was sitting on the edge of the desk right in front of me. "You're here, having missed curfew, smelling like a brewery, and lying to me about drinking."

"That doesn't mean I have a drinking problem!"

He gave me a look that left no doubt he was questioning that. "I want you to know, son, that if you ever need to talk about this, not just here, but any time, you can just call."

I almost blurted out, "I have nothing to talk about," but I knew better. "Thank you, sir. I appreciate that."

I'd heard similar words from different people—teachers and guidance counsellors, mostly—over the years, offering me help with one thing or another. I'd learned that talk was cheap.

"Alcohol is often a problem with hockey players . . . a big problem. I've lived it and I've seen it. If I can help you or anybody else, well, that's my duty."

"Thank you," I repeated, unable to think of anything else to say.

"It's hard to grow up with an alcoholic parent. I know about that too," he said.

Wow! Somehow my father's drinking had finally worked in my favour! It looked like he was going to let me get away with this. I started to get up.

"Now we just have to figure out what to do about you missing curfew and this underage drinking."

I slumped back down. The only luck I ever had was bad.

"In the long run, it wouldn't be fair to you to brush this under the carpet. What do *you* think I should do?"

I shook my head. I had no real idea, and I figured "Leave me alone" wasn't the answer he was looking for.

"I do know that everything starts with being honest . . . including the punishment. So tell me what happened tonight, and remember, I'm pretty good at telling when somebody is lying to me."

Great. If I told him the truth, I'd be betraying Coach Connors . . . and turning my back on my whole future. But there wasn't much choice. I'd have to tell the truth . . . well, at least part of the truth.

"I'm sorry, sir. I admit it. I was drinking. I had four beers . . . no, five. I shouldn't have had any, but I drank too much . . . I'm not used to drinking."

"Let's hope you *don't* get used to it. Now, there's no way that any bar in town would serve you, so where did the beer come from?" he asked.

"Sir, you're putting me in a bad place," I said. That was no lie. "I know I'm in trouble, and I deserve to be in trouble, it's just that I can't tell you . . . I can't rat out somebody else."

"Is it another one of the players at our camp?" he asked.

"No, sir, it isn't." It wasn't a player. "I just don't want to get *her* in any trouble." That was just one word of a lie.

He leaned forward and placed a hand on my shoulder.

"I guess there's honour in protecting a girl. You wouldn't be the first guy who thought with his groin instead of his head. Let's call it a night."

"Thanks, sir." I got up and went for the door.

"We'll meet tomorrow and I'll let you know what your punishment is going to be," he said.

Hopes dashed again. "What could happen?" I asked.

"You could be expelled and sent home."

I felt sick again, but this time it had nothing to do with beer.

"We'll talk tomorrow."

"Thanks, sir."

"Get to sleep," he said.

· · ·

The night passed slowly, without much sleep. For starters, the guys wouldn't let me drift off until I'd told them all about what had happened between me and my imaginary date. She was a lot better looking than any girl I'd ever actually gone out with. Not to mention a lot more accommodating. I'd never gotten that lucky with a real girl.

The next morning, the door to the coaches' office was open. Coach Terry was at his desk and Coach Connors was sitting in a chair next to it.

"Come in," Coach Terry said. "And close the door."

I sat down.

"How are you feeling this morning?" Terry asked.

"Good . . . fine . . . really sorry."

"And your head. Do you have a hangover?" Terry asked.

"No, I'm good," I lied. "Ready to play."

"Whether you'll be able to play hasn't been determined," he said ominously. "The first thing I did this morning was talk to Coach Connors about what happened. He was very disappointed in you."

"Very," Coach Connors said solemnly.

I looked at him closely. He did look disappointed. Was he disappointed that I'd been caught? Had he said anything to Terry to explain what happened?

"Your decision to drink reflects badly on him," Terry continued.

My decision. It was Coach Connors's decision, his beer, and his insisting that I drink to begin with.

"I wanted Coach Connors here this morning since it is because of him that you're even here at this camp."

Both at the camp and in trouble.

"I think we should start with you apologizing to Coach Connors."

I almost laughed but caught myself. I was going to have to apologize to the person who'd got me into trouble to begin with? But what choice did I have?

"I'm sorry . . . really sorry," I said.

"I believe you," Coach Connors answered. "And I want you to know that I accept your apology."

He came forward and offered me his hand. We shook, and then, with his back still turned to Terry, he winked at me. He sat back down.

"You have a good friend in Coach Connors," Terry said. "He is the one who should be most upset and disappointed in you, perhaps the one who should most want you punished, but instead he's spent the morning defending you."

I appreciated that. A lot. My father had never defended me. Although, really, was Coach defending me or protecting himself?

"He told me about your circumstances," Terry said.

What did he mean by that?

"You and I talked about the home situation, so I know about your father, but Coach Connors also told me about the difficulties in school, the impulse issues around temper and fighting. He convinced me that we shouldn't go with a *death sentence* and kick you out of camp."

A wave of relief washed over me.

"In fact, we're not even going to call home to inform your parents of what happened." He looked at Coach Connors, who nodded sympathetically. "Coach Connors felt your father would overreact, possibly take it out on you."

"Thanks, really, thanks."

"Instead, as punishment, you are not allowed to leave the building unless you're under the supervision of a coach. Do you understand?"

"I understand and I'm grateful. Thanks for giving me another chance. I won't let you down . . . again."

"We're counting on that. Now go, get breakfast, and get suited up and ready to play."

I got to my feet and shook hands with both men.

"This is for you," Terry said as he pressed something into my hand. "It's my business card. It has my e-mail and my office phone number. And on the back are my home and cell numbers."

I turned it over. There in pen were two phone numbers.

"I don't know where you're going to be next year, but this is more than just about you as a hockey player. This is about you as a *person*." He paused. "If you need me, you call. I'm only a phone call away."

More empty words.

"Thanks . . . thanks so much."

I tucked the card into my pocket.

"There are lots of things to consider. It's not about making mistakes," he said. "It's about what we learn from those mistakes."

"I've learned, sir, and I won't do it again."

"I'd like to believe you. Go and have breakfast and I'll see you out on the ice."

Coach Connors followed me out of the office and closed the door behind him.

"He still likes you," Coach said.

"That's good . . . although I'm not sure he likes me that much."

"He likes you enough not to kick you out of camp. You know, he's like an institution around here . . . there are lots of snakes in this business, but he has integrity. That's why we're such good friends."

"So he meant what he said about me calling?" I asked.

"He meant it." He paused. "But remember, he's a pretty busy guy, and talking to him about problems might work against you the next time. So . . . just play it cool."

"That's what I figured."

"Besides, it's not like you have a drinking problem . . . other than your father's drinking."

That sounded right to me.

Coach threw an arm around my shoulders as we walked down the hall. "You know I had no choice," he said. "I couldn't tell him."

"I know."

"You handled that well," he said. "I want you to know that I appreciated what you said, and more importantly, what you *didn't* say."

"I've never finked out on anybody in my whole life. I know when to keep my mouth shut," I said.

"What I learned this morning is that I can really trust you. I hope you learned the same thing about me. As far as I'm concerned, this morning, in that office, you just moved up a whole draft position. I'm going to make *sure* you're on my team next year."

CHAPTER NINE

I sat on the couch at home in my living room, trying to focus on the TV and trying not to think about the time. Of course, that was basically impossible. The ticking of the game clock kept me aware that time was passing and I still hadn't received the call. *The call.* That made it seem so casual, a phone call. No big deal. The phone rang all day long. But this was different. It was more important than any phone call I had ever received in my life, maybe more important than anything that had ever happened to me in my whole life. Yet each passing minute meant that I was slipping lower and lower in the draft—maybe nobody was even going to draft me at all.

Coach had called first thing in the morning to reassure me again that he was going to take me in the draft. I was guaranteed to be on his team—unless somebody else drafted me first. That wouldn't be what I wanted, but it wouldn't be so bad . . . would it? I'd still be playing Junior A, just not for him. I'd have to hope that the other coach really wanted me and it wasn't just a pick made by his GM. And then I'd have to hope that my new coach was good, and that he liked me, and that I'd get playing time, and . . . it would be so much easier if it was Coach Connors. Everybody knew how good he was, but more important, he knew how good I was—how good I could become.

My mother had mentioned to me that having him as my coach would be like having a "father figure." I knew what she thought that meant, but the last thing I wanted was for anybody else to act like my father did.

Almost on cue, my father walked into the room, holding a beer. He looked at his watch and then at me. He didn't need to say what he was thinking, but I knew that wasn't going to stop him.

"Figured there'd be a call by now," he said. "Assuming there's going to be a call."

"There's going to be a call," I said, trying to sound confident, trying to convince both of us.

I knew he'd be disappointed if I wasn't drafted—nothing to brag about at the bar—but I also knew there was another part of him that almost would have welcomed it. Misery loves company. If he couldn't make it, then he didn't want me to make it either. It wasn't anything he said—I just knew the sort of person he was.

"Nothing is done until it's done," I said. "Coach promised me."

My father snorted. "Promises don't mean nothing. People say things all the time, but talk don't mean anything. Haven't I taught you nothing?"

He'd taught me a lot. You could learn almost as much from a bad example as you could from a good one.

"Coach is going to call," I insisted.

"It wasn't that many years ago that I was some hotshot kid thinking I was going to be a pro, thinking I was going to get the call, get the chance . . . and now?" He shrugged. "I'm just some worn-out bum in a dead-end job who drinks too much."

I was shocked. That was probably the most honest thing I'd ever heard him say. He did know. Maybe that was why he *did* drink so much.

"Not that that is necessarily gonna happen to you, kid . . . you're a talented hockey player," he said.

Honest *and* caring. Where did that come from? How much had he had to drink?

"You better hope he calls, though, because hockey is all you got going for you," he snapped.

He was right. It wasn't just that it was the only thing I was good at, it was the only dream I had, the only chance I had. Out there on the ice was the only place I really felt good, and I wanted that feeling to keep happening. I didn't want to become some bitter, drunken bum in a do-nothing job, boring everybody with his stories about what might have been, how he'd been robbed, how he could have been in the Show. I felt almost ill thinking about it, about becoming *him.*

The phone rang and both my father and I jumped. It rang a second time.

"You gonna get that?" he asked.

I got up. What if it was just somebody trying to sell us new windows, or air duct cleaning, or—

"Get the phone!" my father ordered.

I picked it up. "Hello?"

"Hello, Cody!"

"Hey, Coach."

I looked over at my father as my mother came out of the kitchen and stood beside him, drying her hands on a tea towel.

"You know what this phone call is about. As promised, I'm calling to offer my congratulations on you being drafted," Coach said.

"Thank you." I tried to keep my voice calm, my face neutral. In some ways it was easy, because, even hearing it, I didn't necessarily believe it.

I gave my parents a nod and a thumbs-up, and then allowed myself a small smile. They both burst into big smiles and hugged each other. It was an awkward hug.

"I'm calling to formally tell you that you have been

drafted by the Watertown Warriors. Are you willing to play for me?" he asked.

"Are you kidding? Yes!"

"That's great to hear. We'll talk details later, and, of course, we have to arrange for a billet, the family you'll live with next season. We'll find you a good home."

"I'll live with anybody, anywhere. It doesn't matter. I just want to play hockey."

"I'll make sure you're living with a nice family. You might be the only player there, or there might be one or two other players, if that's what you want. Maybe you'll want to share with Josh."

"So you drafted him too? That's great," I said, hoping I sounded convincing. I wasn't even sure I wanted him around. He was really skilled, and too much competition wasn't necessarily the best thing when you were trying to land a job and get ice time.

"I was lucky to get him. I don't think he would have lasted another pick, and he certainly wouldn't have lasted to the next round," Coach said.

"Did he go first round?" I asked.

"Fourth pick in the first round."

"And me?" I asked, blurting it out before I thought about maybe not wanting to know the answer.

"Fourth round."

"Oh," I mumbled. "I thought I'd go, you know, higher."

"Don't be disappointed. It isn't the round that you go that matters, it's that you were drafted that matters. You think anybody remembers that Mark Messier was drafted in the third round?"

"He was?"

"How about Dino Ciccarelli and his 1,200 points, or Stumpy Thomas with 933 points in twenty NHL seasons, or Adam Oates with 1,420 points?"

"You mean they weren't drafted high either?"

"Lots of players weren't drafted into the Show, or came into Junior A un-drafted, and went on to NHL careers. Don't sweat it."

"I won't . . . it's just that I thought you or somebody else was going to take me higher than that."

"It was a gamble on my part, but not a big one. If somebody else had drafted you, I would have worked out a deal to get you back," he said.

"You would have?"

"I know how good you are, and—more important— how good you're going to be. The reason you sank lower had nothing to do with your skills," he said.

"Then what *did* it have to do with?"

"Some of the scouts questioned your character. There were the problems at school, and then the whole incident at the camp . . . you know, being out after curfew and being caught intoxicated."

Terry—he must have told one of the other coaches or somebody outside the organization. It was just more proof of what Coach kept saying—the hockey world was a small one and everybody was connected. If Terry had really wanted to help me, he would have kept his mouth shut.

"You were the steal of the entire draft," he said. "I *know* what sort of person you are. You now have a chance to show them just how wrong they were. Use your disappointment and your anger as fuel, as motivation."

"I don't need any more motivation. I'm going to prove them all wrong."

"And you're going to make me look like a genius. I'm going to give you every chance. You're going to spend some time on the power play, on penalty kill, and you'll start right off as the second line centre."

I didn't question why only the second line centre. I'd show everyone that the first line was where I belonged.

"The important thing is that you've been drafted. You're going to play Junior A, and you're going to be on *my* team. You're *my* player."

"You're right," I said. "Thanks, thanks for everything. And could you thank Terry too?"

There was silence. "I maybe shouldn't be saying this, but Terry is one of those people you have to prove wrong."

I guess he didn't just talk bad about me, he thought bad about me.

"Not that he disagreed with having you on the team," Coach said. "And he certainly didn't question my choice. It's just that he thought you could have been taken with a later pick."

Great. I had an owner who wanted me but thought I wasn't worth the price they paid.

"Believe me, you're going to prove him wrong too. Now put your father or mother on the phone so I can give them my formal congratulations."

"Okay. And Coach . . . I won't disappoint you."

"I know you won't . . . I know you won't."

CHAPTER TEN

We pulled up to the motel, and Coach stopped the car at the front door—the office.

"I'll get the rooms. Why don't you boys grab yourself something cool to drink," he suggested. He handed me a five-dollar bill.

"Thanks, sure."

He headed into the office while Josh and Jake and I climbed out. We walked over to the pop machine. The motel looked practically deserted.

"Man, is it ever hot," Jake said.

Jake was one of the other players drafted by Coach. There were four new players, and three of us were on this six-day road trip to and from Watertown. The season wouldn't start for another month, but Coach wanted us to meet the principal of the high school we'd be attending, spend some time with our billet family, and just get to know the town better. It made sense to be prepared because he said there would be so many new things. Advance planning like this was typical for Coach. He was always looking ahead, always doing the little things to make sure everything went well. Already he was drilling it into us that he didn't just have a plan, he had a backup plan, and a backup for the backup.

I straightened the bill out and inserted it into the drink machine. It slid right back out. I turned it around the right way and put it in again. This time it took the money. I pressed the button for a Coke, and the machine whizzed and clicked and a can thudded into the bottom.

"This is all cool," Jake said. "It's like our first team trip, but with only part of the team."

"And with no ice, no games, and boiling hot weather," Josh added. "So, what was it like sharing a room with Coach last night?"

"He snores," Jake said. "Sounds like a bear . . . a bear that swallowed a chainsaw. I guess one of you will find out tonight," Jake said.

Four separate rooms would have been too expensive, so we were sharing two rooms, rotating roommates each night. Coach said it would give us a chance to get to know each other better.

"I'll flip you to see who gets him tonight," Josh said as he pulled a quarter out of his pocket.

"No need to flip. He's all yours," I suggested.

"I was thinking loser has to take him."

"Then Jake should get every night," I said.

"Funny, very funny."

"The truth is seldom pretty, but it's deadly serious," I replied.

Coach came out of the office. "Okay, we're checked in. Josh and Jake, you're bunk mates tonight, and Cody, you're with me."

Josh smirked, and when Coach turned his back, he mimed starting up a chainsaw. I would have been angry if it hadn't been so funny. Besides, his turn would come tomorrow.

"The motel is almost completely booked, so the two rooms are on opposite sides of the compound." He handed Josh a key. "Get your things in your room and then come and find us. We're in room 154."

They grabbed their bags out of the car and I got into the passenger seat. As they walked off in one direction, we drove off in the other. We turned around the side of the motel and drove along the back. There were no cars there either. The other guests must have already been out, or maybe they had made reservations and were checking in later.

"There's our room," Coach said. He pulled the car up in front.

We gathered our overnight bags and he opened the door and went in, flicking on the light. It wasn't much of a room: dingy, bad lighting, with brown carpet and . . .

"I know, there's only the one bed," Coach said.

It had stopped surprising me when he knew what I was thinking. He always seemed to know what people were thinking—not just me, but *everybody*. He said that dealing with people was like playing chess—it was important that you were always thinking three steps ahead.

"I tried to get twin beds in each room, like the last place, but the only rooms left had just one bed. I'll sleep on the couch," he offered.

"I could sleep on the couch."

"It's not that big a deal . . . my back has been much better the last year or so . . . old injury flares up sometimes."

"Then you definitely need to sleep on the bed."

He shook his head. "I'd feel guilty. Besides, I can't let it get around that I take kids on road trips and make them sleep on a couch."

I looked at the couch and then at the bed. The couch was tiny and the bed was huge, maybe even a queen size.

"It is a big bed. We could share it."

"Aren't you worried about my snoring?" he asked. "I've been told it's pretty loud."

"I don't think the extra five feet between the bed and couch is going to make much difference."

"Well . . . I don't know," he said.

"Please, that way I won't feel guilty."

"Deal, and I'll let you choose the side," Coach said.

It really didn't matter much to me. I guess it really didn't make much difference, and it was only for the night. Besides, it wasn't like I hadn't shared a bed before. I took my bag and tossed it on the bed and it landed more on the right than the left—that was *my* side.

There was a knock and I turned to see the guys at the open door.

"That was fast," Coach said.

"We're starving," Josh said.

"Yeah, can we eat soon?" Jake asked.

"For sure." He turned to me. "Cody, tonight you get to pick the spot where we eat."

• • •

"That was good," Josh said.

"It was big," Jake added.

"That's what made it so good," Josh replied.

We'd each had a couple of burgers, home fries, and the soft drink was bottomless. I was now highly carbonated.

Coach waved for the waitress. She came over and he pulled out a big wad of bills. I could see by her reaction that she was both surprised and impressed. I was still impressed, but I wasn't surprised anymore. He always had lots of money on him. He handed her the cash.

"I'll be back with the change," she said.

"Don't be silly, honey. You keep it."

"Thank you," she exclaimed. She walked away beaming.

"I always pay in cash," he said. "That way, the waitress gets to keep her share and she doesn't have to split it with the government. As well, unless the service is crummy, you should give a good tip . . . around fifteen percent. Remember that, especially if you make it to the Show. Be generous, and always be kind, because people are watching you all the time. Tip crummy and it might end up on YouTube. You just remember that for a lot of people, you're their hero, their role model, so behave accordingly."

I *loved* when he talked about the Show. It made it seem more real, more possible.

We got up to leave.

"Thanks for coming!" the waitress sang out, waved, and gave us a big smile.

"Like I said, people remember, take note, when you treat them well," Coach said.

"I'd like the chance to treat *her* well," Josh said.

"It's good to have a dream, but I think she's a little out of your age bracket," Coach said. "But there are lots of girls in Watertown. They're going to be *all* over the three of you. You're going to have to fight them off with a hockey stick."

"I'm not planning on fighting that hard," Jake said. Josh gave him a high-five. The two of them seemed to be getting on really well, making me feel like I was on the outside. Nothing new there.

I knew there'd be time for girls, but I wasn't going to let some puck-bunnies get in the way of what I needed to do and where I was going. Coach had said that to me a couple of times, and I didn't need to be told many things more than once . . . well . . . if I thought they were right.

We walked outside and along the street to where we'd parked our car. There weren't that many vehicles in the lot, but one of the few, a big pickup truck, was tucked in tightly beside us.

"A whole parking lot and this donkey had to park right here," Coach said.

He tried to squeeze between the two vehicles, swearing under his breath. He brushed against both of them as he moved.

"Look, he's so tight I probably won't even be able to open my door."

He unlocked it and opened it, banging his door against the truck with a loud thud. He then did it again and again, the sound of the door hitting against the truck echoing throughout the parking lot, getting louder each time as he hit it harder.

"You can get in through the passenger side," Josh offered.

"I could, but not yet," Coach exclaimed. "I'm not through with this guy yet!"

His face was bright red and he was looking mad enough to spit. He stomped back toward the street. What was he going to do? Was he going to try to find the guy?

"Should we go with him?" Jake asked a bit nervously.

"I don't think . . ."

Coach stopped beside a newspaper box. Suddenly he picked it up and lifted it over his head! I couldn't believe that he could do that! The thing had to weigh a ton. But why would he . . . ? He started to carry it back.

"What is he doing?" Jake said.

There was only one reason I could think of. He carried it over and then he dropped the newspaper box onto the hood of the truck! It landed with a thunderous crash!

Josh and Jake jumped in shock. I'd seen it coming, so I wasn't completely surprised. I looked all around. There was nobody around to see or hear what he'd done—thank goodness. There was no way that the hood hadn't been scratched or dented or damaged in some way.

"*Now* we can go," Coach said.

Quickly we all climbed into the car and drove away.

"I hate rude jerks," Coach said. "They get me so angry . . . sometimes my temper gets the better of me." He paused. "But I bet he won't park that close to somebody again!"

Coach started laughing and we all joined in.

"Aren't you afraid that you could get in trouble if you got caught?" Josh asked.

"I'm not worried. I've already gotten to know some of the police around Watertown and they know the police in this town. A Junior A coach is a big thing in a town like this, even if it's not his town . . . If they did make a fuss, I'd make sure to give them extra tickets for games, get things signed for their kids. I've always done that wherever

I've coached . . . I've tried to develop an *understanding*," he said.

He did seem to know everybody, and to go out of his way to get to know the people he needed to know.

What had surprised me was the anger. Not just what he'd done but how such a little thing had triggered it, how big it got, and then, almost instantly, how it was gone. It was something I could see my father doing, but there was a big difference. With my father, there was always a slow buildup, and then he took a long, long time to cool down. With Coach, both sides of the mountain had been steep.

"We have one more stop," Coach said. "I was thinking we should get a case of beer to bring back to the motel . . . unless, of course, you gentlemen don't drink."

Both Josh and Jake protested that they'd had "a beer or two" before.

"And since Cody chose such a good place for dinner, I'll leave it up to him to choose the type of beer. You're partial to Canadian, as I recall."

CHAPTER ELEVEN

I'd like to propose a toast," Coach said. "To the three newest members of the Watertown Warriors. You will form the core of the team that will ultimately lead us to the championship!"

We all cheered and clinked our bottles together, and then I tipped mine back and drained it. I put the empty on the table beside the others. Among the four of us we'd almost killed the entire 2–4. I grabbed another beer.

"Do you really think we can win it all?" Josh asked.

"Don't you?" Coach said.

"Yeah, sure . . . of course," he mumbled.

"Not very convincing. How about you, Cody, what do you think?"

"I don't *think*. I *know*. We're going to win it all!"

"That's what I like to hear!" Coach yelled. "A toast to Cody!"

We tapped bottles together again and chugged.

"Cody's got a lot of confidence for a fourth-round pick," Jake said.

He'd already made a few comments about how he was second round and I was only fourth. He'd never seen me play and I'd never seen him play. I imagined he was probably pretty good, but he just assumed that he was two rounds better than me.

I was starting to fantasize about him being on another team so I could beat a little sense into him. Then again, during training camp it was pretty much okay to mix it up with somebody on your team. Nobody would object to one rookie hammering away on another. It would not only feel good, it would establish me as a guy nobody should mess with.

Josh started laughing for no apparent reason. He was a giggly drunk—which was better than Jake, who was more the loud and obnoxious type. If I'd wanted to be around a loud and obnoxious drunk, I would have stayed home. Funny thing, the guy had only put away three beers. The jerk couldn't handle his alcohol at all.

Coach sat in the corner, smiling, laughing, and telling us stories, making us all laugh. I kept thinking that he was part of a tribe of hockey men that stretched all the way back to Gordie Howe, and the Rocket, and even before that. And we were being auditioned to be part of that tribe. This was the beginning, the opening, the way in. This was like the best day of my life.

"We'd better call it a night," Coach said. "We have to leave early tomorrow."

Josh and Jake got up. Jake stumbled and practically fell over before he regained his balance.

"Do you think you two can find your way back to your room without an escort?" Coach asked.

"We're okay," Josh said.

After they'd left, Josh propping Jake up as he wobbled out the door, Coach told me, "I've got to keep my eye on Jake. Kid is young and can't handle his alcohol. You really want to pop him one, don't you?"

Once again he was reading my mind—or the look on my face. "I've thought about it. If he keeps shooting off his mouth, he may find my fist in it."

"You've got to learn to control your temper," Coach said.

"I guess we could both do with learning that," I said, the words rushing out before I realized what I was saying. Was he going to hate me?

He just sighed. "That was not my finest moment, back there outside the restaurant."

I was relieved. And I figured it wasn't too late to recover. "No, he deserved it, and you were right."

"I just don't like it when people cross me," he said.

"Yeah, I'm not so crazy about that myself."

"Let's work on that together. Of course, on the ice it's important that you don't lose that nasty edge. Just pick your spots, right?"

"I'll try."

"Maybe I understand you so well because I understand how hard that can be sometimes. When people tick you off, you can show them on the ice. Don't worry, it won't be long before training camp starts." He walked over and put his hands on my shoulders. "You know that *I* believe in you . . . that I think you're special."

I didn't know what to say, so I just sort of shrugged.

"It's time for bed, but first things first." He pulled out the last two bottles from the case. "No beer left behind. We have to finish these."

"I'm still working on this one," I said, holding up my bottle.

"I have a solution. Bottoms up."

He tipped up his bottle and I did the same, draining it. I'd hardly put the bottle down when he handed me the new one.

"I'm impressed that you can handle your drink," Coach said. "Lots of kids come to Junior A and they get into trouble with alcohol. There's always going to be a few beers around after a game."

I'd had a lot more than a few beers.

"You boys walk into a bar or restaurant and there will be people wanting to buy you a drink. You don't want to offend them by refusing, so you can't avoid it. The important thing is to know how to handle it. I know *you* can handle it."

He clinked his bottle against mine.

"And just as important, I know I can trust you," he continued.

He tipped back his bottle and I did the same, chugging it. When I got up I felt a little rush. Maybe I wasn't handling this as well as either of us thought I was. Either way, it would only help me sleep better tonight—maybe I wouldn't notice him snoring.

• • •

My eyes popped open, but I couldn't see anything in the pitch-black. There was a weight on my chest and—

"Stop struggling . . . take it easy."

It was Coach's voice.

He was on top of me. His weight was pinning me down and his hands were holding my arms in place!

"What are you doing?" I gasped.

"You know what I'm doing . . . you're the one who invited me into the bed . . . remember?" he whispered. "Just lie still . . . don't say a word . . . and just enjoy."

My mind raced, trying to make sense of what was happening. He let go of my arms, and I felt his hands moving all over me in places they should never have been. I wanted to push him off, scream out for him to stop, tell him I wasn't like that, to do something, do anything. But I couldn't. It wasn't like it was real—it *couldn't* be real. Was I dreaming . . . hallucinating . . . was this from all the alcohol? No, this was real.

I felt like my mind and body were paralyzed, unable to move, unable to speak, even if I could have found words to say. Nothing made sense. My head was spinning and I closed my eyes so tight that I couldn't even see his outline above me. I tried to remove myself, make my mind go somewhere else . . . get away from it all. I wanted to cry, or at least cry out, but I couldn't. Instead I felt my mind drift away from my body, floating up and away. Even hovering above I kept my eyes closed tightly so I couldn't look down from the ceiling and see what was going on. I needed to forget it even while it was still happening.

CHAPTER TWELVE

Little bits of light leaked in from around the curtains. It was morning. Somehow I'd managed to get to sleep, or had I finally just passed out again from the alcohol? I startled at the sound of water running in the bathroom, and then the door opened up and light flooded into the room.

"Time to get up, sleepyhead!" Coach called out cheerfully.

I sat up in bed. My head was hurting, but more than hurting, it was filled with thoughts—confusing, awful, terrible thoughts.

"You need to get up and take a shower. I'm going to grab breakfast for everybody for the drive . . . you okay with an Egg McMuffin meal?"

"Yeah, sure," I mumbled.

"Great!" he exclaimed. "I'll be back in fifteen. You have to be washed, dressed, packed, and waiting outside by the front office. You return the key, okay?"

"The key?"

"To the room. It's on the dresser. I already have my bag with me." He paused. "Are you okay?"

How could I be okay? "Yeah."

"Great. See you at the car. And remember, fifteen minutes. We'll be waiting."

The door closed behind him—locking as it closed—with the key on the dresser. I was alone and he couldn't get back in. Slowly I climbed out of bed. My legs felt shaky and my stomach was upset. I saw the phone on the nightstand. I should call somebody and tell them . . . but who? Who should I call? My mind raced around and came up with no answer. I certainly couldn't call my father, and it wasn't like my mother would or could do anything without him. Besides, what would I even say to her? What would I say to anybody?

I staggered into the bathroom and closed the door behind me—locking it. I climbed out of the clothes I'd slept in and turned on the shower. Once the hot water was running over my head and down my body, I grabbed the little bar of soap and ripped the wrapper open with my teeth. I lathered it up and started scrubbing away. I just felt so awful . . . so dirty . . . so sick to my stomach. My stomach violently convulsed and I threw up. Clear, yellowish, alcohol-smelling vomit bounced off the bottom of the shower stall and up onto my legs, instantly washed away by the water flowing down.

I leaned against the wall, my stomach still heaving, my legs still shaking, and just stood there and let the water continue to wash over me. I just wanted the water to wash everything away.

It all spun around in my head again. It was like a terrible memory—no, not a memory, because it wasn't like it had actually happened to *me*. It was more like I had seen it on TV, or in a movie . . . no, wrong again . . . more like I'd heard it all on the radio, because my eyes had been so tightly closed and the room so dark that I couldn't see anything. But I could still feel it. Feel the weight on my chest, feel hands on my—my stomach convulsed and I threw up again.

The only thing churning faster than my stomach was my head, trying to make sense of it . . . it did happen . . . right? It wasn't a dream . . . no, not a dream, a nightmare. A nightmare that was real.

• • •

I circled around the side of the motel. Coach's Escalade was parked there and the three of them were leaning against it, waiting. It had been a lot longer than fifteen minutes. They were all talking loudly and there was lots of laughter. I couldn't help but think—did what happened to me happen to Jake that first night? No, it couldn't have. At least, Jake didn't act like anything had happened . . . but wasn't that how I was trying to act?

"You're late," Coach said.

"What were you doing, fixing your makeup?" Josh asked.

"What did you say?" I snapped.

"Um . . . nothing . . . just joking around, man."

"Yeah, chill out," Jake said. "I told them you were late because you were a late pick in the draft and—"

I dropped my bag and barrelled into Jake, smashing him against the car, and then we both fell into the dirt of the driveway, swinging and kicking as we hit the ground! I connected with a solid shot to the jaw and he screamed in pain. Before he could react, I hit him a second time and a third and—

"Stop it, now!" Coach yelled.

He reached down and grabbed me by the arm and with incredible power yanked me up and away as I still tried to get in a final lick at Jake. Jake staggered to his feet, his hands holding his nose but not the blood flowing out of it.

"You got anything more you want to say?" I screamed.

"You idiot!" he yelled back, his voice muffled by his hands.

"You calling me an idiot? You want some more?" I hollered, trying to break free of Coach, but he held me back, my arms pinned behind me.

"Both of you stop!" he yelled. "Listen to me now or else! Stop talking and stop struggling!"

I did what he said, easing off, and then he released his grip.

"That's better. Now both of you, sit down . . . right there on the hood of the car."

I sat. Jake did the same, just not right beside me.

"First things first," Coach said. "Jake, you need to apologize to Cody."

"Me apologize to him!" he exclaimed as he jumped off the car.

I jumped up as well, ready for him to take a swing at me. Instead he moved a few feet away. He was afraid. "He was the one who attacked me!" he yelled.

"And he'll apologize for that, but you need to apologize first because you started it all by shooting off your mouth. If you hadn't been yapping, he wouldn't have been swinging."

Jake didn't say anything at first. I figured there was no way he wanted to apologize, but he didn't really have much choice.

"I didn't mean anything," he finally said. "I was just joking around."

"Is that supposed to be an apology?" I asked.

He shrugged. "I'm sorry."

"Now you," Coach said to me.

"I shouldn't have punched you . . . so many times . . . sorry about your nose."

"That's better," Coach said. "Now shake hands and remember you're teammates."

Jake offered me his hand first. It was covered in blood—his blood, that I'd caused to flow. I hesitated. I think everybody was holding their breath, wondering if I was going to take his hand. I wondered myself. Finally, we shook. It didn't mean anything.

"Cody, if somebody pounded Jake into the boards in a game, what would you do?" Coach asked.

"Celebrate" is what I wanted to say, but I knew the right answer. "I'd jump the guy and beat the hell out of him."

"Why?" Coach asked.

"He's my teammate, and that's what teammates do," I explained.

Coach nodded his head. "I knew you'd say that. This all ends here and now. Josh, take Jake inside the motel office and get some ice for his nose."

They started off, leaving us alone.

"I know you're upset . . . and confused," he said. "About last night."

Suddenly him saying it, now, out here in the light of day, made it seem more real and less real all at once. He was looking right at me. I looked away, ashamed.

"And maybe some of that confusion is what fuelled you lashing out at Jake . . . not that he didn't deserve it. I want you to know that if you say the word, he's gone."

"What?"

"If you want him off the team, he's off the team. I'll trade him or just release him or sit him on the end of the bench until he quits."

"You'd do that?"

"I can do *whatever* I want. Whatever *you* want. I'm the coach. If you don't want him on our team, then he's gone. As soon as we get back home, I'll tell him I made a mistake drafting him."

I shook my head. "No . . . it's okay."

"As long as you're okay with him, he can stay." He placed a hand on my shoulder. I tried to lean away but I couldn't. He held me firmly in place.

"You know what I think of you as a player. What I think of you as a person. You have to know that you can trust me the same way I can trust you. And trust is one of the key things I need from my captain."

"Captain . . . you're going to make me the captain?"

"Not this year. There is a captain. He's a fourth-year player . . . his final year. Next year he's gone and I think you'll make a great captain. You know the NHL scouts look at that, they draft leaders, they draft captains. That's the goal, to get to the Show, and I can help you, the way I've helped others."

Did he help the others the way he helped me? Was it like last night? I wanted his help—no, I *needed* his help—to get where I wanted to go, but did that mean it was going to happen again?

"You just have to do what I say." He shook me slightly.

"Look at me," he said, his voice suddenly more serious, more forceful.

I looked up, but I had trouble meeting his gaze.

"You know you're special to me."

What could I say to that? He was my coach, my ticket to the Show, one of the few people in my life who had ever treated me right—he was special to me too, just not in *that* way. How could I tell him that without risking everything?

"Just remember, I have the power to decide whether Jake . . . or *anybody* else . . . has a chance to make it. It all comes down to me."

What he was saying was true.

"So, Cody . . . Captain Cody . . . can I count on you?"

I took a deep breath and then nodded my head. What choice did I have?

CHAPTER THIRTEEN

I shifted uneasily in my seat. Coach sat beside me in the booth. Meetings with principals were never happy occasions, and even though it was summer and we were in a restaurant and the guy was dressed in shorts, I didn't expect this one to be any different. The principal had already sat down with Josh and Jake, and I had no illusions that Coach was saving the best for last. Josh had said it was "no sweat" when he came out, but Coach had told me that he was a really good student. Apparently he was as much a golden boy off the ice as he was on it. Another reason to dislike him.

In some ways it would have been better if I had gone before Jake. The principal must have asked him about his face. It had stopped bleeding hours earlier, during the car ride here, but it still looked like somebody had mugged him. Maybe the principal hadn't asked, or maybe Jake had actually kept his mouth shut about how it happened. Actually, judging from the silent treatment Jake had given me on the five-hour car ride, the only chance of him keeping quiet was if he was afraid of me. He had *reason* to be afraid of me.

Finally, after studying my student record, the principal, Mr. Paisley, looked up at me. He smiled, although it didn't look like a real smile.

"So, Cody, do you believe in fresh starts?" he asked.

"I guess I'd better."

He laughed. "I guess we'd *all* better," he said. "This is certainly not a record to be proud of."

"Believe me, I'm not proud of it, sir."

"That's good to hear. Some people do pride themselves on being tough guys. There are lots of notations on your record about fighting. Do you see yourself as a tough guy?"

"I can take care of myself," I said, and then thought better of it. "But really, I see myself as more of a stupid guy who gets into stupid fights about nothing without thinking."

"Like today?" he asked.

"Like today," I replied. So much for Jake keeping his mouth shut. But what did I expect? If he'd kept his mouth shut to begin with, none of this would have happened.

"Impulse control seems to be an issue," Mr. Paisley said.

"Not to excuse what happened today," Coach said, "but he didn't really start it. He kept his temper the first half-dozen times he was provoked . . . not that he was *right* in finally reacting the way he did."

"I appreciate that you tried to control yourself, but you're going to have to try harder," the principal said. "Fighting on school property is an automatic suspension for both parties."

"What if I didn't start it and only swung back?" I asked.

"*Both* parties. If somebody swings at you, then you are to come down to the office and report them," Mr. Paisley said.

"Yeah, I can see how that would work," I mumbled sarcastically.

"It *does* work." He paused. "I know that it's different from what happens in hockey. I've played a little shinny in my time, and I was pretty good, if I do say so myself."

I wanted to say, "Yeah, right, that's why you're a principal," but I didn't. At least I had *some* impulse control.

"And I know that out there on the ice, you have to take care of yourself. You have to be a tough guy. If somebody drops the gloves, you have no choice but to answer the bell. But *you* have to understand that I'm running a school and not an arena. Here you have to be tough enough *not* to fight back."

"You're exactly right," Coach said. "School requires an altogether different approach to challenges. On the ice, I expect my players to back down from nobody, and believe me, Cody is one of the best—he's a tough-as-nails player—but that's not the right attitude for school. Maybe nobody has ever explained it to him that clearly. I've got to be honest, nobody has ever explained it to *me* that clearly."

I wasn't sure if he was agreeing or simply buttering up the principal to get him on our side.

Coach turned to me. "Cody, do you realize how fortunate we are to have a principal who not only agreed to give up his time during the summer to meet with us, and who understands hockey, but who also understands some issues on a level that I hadn't thought through?" He turned back to Mr. Paisley. "Again, I want you to know how grateful I am."

"It's my pleasure. But perhaps I should be thanking you," he said. "You're the first coach who has ever taken the time to meet with me. You're going above and beyond too."

"I can't imagine why all coaches *wouldn't* do that," Coach said. "We're not just trying to produce hockey players, we're trying to produce well-rounded young men, and that has to include a partnership with the school. We're all on the same team, and in matters surrounding the school, you, sir, are the captain, coach, and owner all rolled into one. I'll do whatever is necessary to help make this partnership a success for *our* boys . . . because they really are *our* boys."

"What a wonderful attitude!" Mr. Paisley beamed. "You know, a lot of the players and coaches for the Warriors have given me the impression that school, for them, was nothing more than an inconvenience that got in the way of hockey."

"That would be incredibly short-sighted," Coach said. "While we hope that some of these boys will move on to professional careers, we all know that the vast majority will not, and without a proper education, they'll have nothing."

"Again, I really appreciate your attitude, Coach. Perhaps I can get out and see a few more games this year."

"That would be wonderful!" Coach exclaimed. "In fact, I'm going to arrange for there to be two complimentary tickets for you at the door for every one of our home games."

"That's . . . that's so generous, so kind of you!"

"They'll be seats right by our bench. I think it would be incredible for the boys to see you there and know you're on their side."

"I *am* on their side. I think the whole town is on their side . . . although I'm not sure how happy the town is going to be with your decision to suspend them from hockey if I suspend them from school."

"What?" I gasped.

Coach looked directly at me. "I've told Principal Paisley that it is *my* decision that if any player is suspended from school, he will also be suspended from the team for the same period."

"Something no coach has ever done before, I might add," Mr. Paisley said.

"It's all about getting the boys to take school more seriously, by reinforcing the lesson, adding consequences for their behaviour," Coach said. "Cody, do you think that will stop you from fighting at school?"

I held up my hands in surrender. "I'm not fighting anybody who isn't wearing a pair of skates."

"Excellent," Mr. Paisley said. "Of course, the other issue for you is around your academics. Your marks are very low, and we also suspend students who fail courses."

"I think that's an important life lesson," Coach said. "Anybody who fails is simply failing to try hard enough."

"Those are my thoughts exactly!" Mr. Paisley exclaimed. "And I want you to know that we have additional help available at the school."

"I'll make sure the boys avail themselves of those services," Coach said. "But with Cody here, I'm going to go the extra mile." He reached over and placed a hand on my shoulder, and I fought not to react to his touch. "I am going to *personally* tutor him. After all, a coach is just a different kind of teacher."

"I wish all coaches—heck, all parents—had your attitude and ideas," Mr. Paisley said.

"And I wish all principals were as dedicated and visionary as you, sir," Coach offered.

"Just doing my job."

"As I am mine," Coach said. "And together, you and I, we can do right by these boys."

I could see what Coach was doing—what he'd *done*.

He had turned this whole thing around. The principal was on our side now—was on *Coach's* side. He just had this way of saying the right things, doing the right thing, so that people couldn't help but like him. I wondered how much of what he'd said he really believed.

"Young man, you are fortunate to have a coach like this," Mr. Paisley said to me. "So often at this level the only thing that a coach cares about is winning and losing. I know that your coach actually cares about you as a person, and that is rare."

"Again, you're being too kind," Coach said. "Cody, is there anything you want to say to your new principal?"

I knew what was expected. "I want to thank you, sir, for all that you've said, and I promise you that I won't let you down. I'll work as hard at school as I will on the ice."

"And we'll work hard for you as well," Mr. Paisley said. "Now, is there anything you want to say to your Coach?"

There were lots of things I wanted to say, wanted to ask, but I knew I couldn't ask any of them. "I guess I just want to say thanks."

He smiled at me. "You know it really is *my* pleasure."

• • •

Later that day, I'd moved from one seat to another, from one place to another. This time, instead of a booth in a restaurant, it was a seat in the living room of a house. And instead of Principal Paisley, it was a whole family—

mother, father, twin eleven-year-old sons, and a baby. They were going to be billeting all three of us during the season. My first thought was about how much I didn't want to live with Jake. The only good thing was that I knew that he wanted to live with me even *less*.

Josh, on the other hand, was being Josh. He was bouncing the baby and talking to the kids and the parents like he was trying to win the audition for adorable older brother. They were all friendly and happy to have us. They seemed like the perfect family, in a Sears catalogue or an Old Navy commercial sort of way.

I shouldn't have been surprised that Josh was just as comfortable with them as they were with us. He'd grown up in a family—a *real* family, the kind with a father and mother and younger sister, where everybody was normal. Not that they couldn't be something different under the surface. I looked over at Coach talking and smiling.

I was having trouble concentrating on the conversation. I'd hardly slept at all the night before, which made it even harder to make sense of everything. My mind kept circling around, looking for an answer, a reason, a solution, a way out, an explanation. But each time it cycled around, I came up with the same answer. My coach—this man who everybody seemed to love, this man who said he wanted only the best for me, this man who held the key to my whole future—had been groping me.

No, that couldn't be true. My mind started the same cycle again. I had to have missed something, or I didn't understand . . . something. I'd been there and I still couldn't believe it . . . not Coach . . . not with me.

"So, Cody, you've been very quiet," Mrs. Olsen said.

"Just thinking," I said. That much wasn't a lie. I was wondering if this was a safe place, if they were good people. I had lots of questions that a brief meeting wouldn't answer. "You really have a beautiful home," I said, knowing they were looking for more.

"Thank you so much. I really hope you'll soon come to think of this as *your* home. I hope all of you boys will," she said.

"I already feel at home," Josh said, eliciting a smile from everybody.

"You still need to see your rooms," Mr. Olsen said. "I'll show them to you."

We got up and followed him down the basement stairs.

"With the exception of the laundry room, you have the basement to yourselves. The bedrooms aren't huge," he said, "but you each have your own. I know how important privacy is to a teenage boy."

From the outside it didn't look like a very large house, but the basement was big. Mr. Olsen pushed open the door to the first room and flicked on the light. It was small, but it did look neat and tidy. The ceiling was partway above ground, so there was a window that let in a lot of light. He showed us the other two rooms. They were basically repeats of the first, just painted in different colours and with different patterned quilts on the beds.

"You three will also be sharing the same bathroom." He pushed open another door to reveal bright lights, a double sink, big mirror, a toilet, tub, and a separate shower stall. "We also make it a rule that our own boys are not allowed downstairs," Mr. Olsen said.

"Oh, they can come down if they want," Josh said. "They won't bother us."

"No," Mr. Olsen said forcefully. "It's important that you have your privacy. We'll make sure our boys respect that."

"And *my* boys will remember that respect goes both ways," Coach said. "Cody, Josh, Jake, while you're living under this roof, you are to give Mr. and Mrs. Olsen your *complete* respect."

We all nodded our heads solemnly.

"Not just here, but in the community," he continued. "This is a small town where everybody knows everybody."

"And gossips about everybody!" Mrs. Olsen added, and then laughed nervously.

"Exactly. What you do out there in the community reflects on this fine family, and I want you to do right by them."

Again we all nodded.

He turned to the Olsens. "My boys will comport themselves as gentlemen. You have my home and cell-phone numbers, and if there's any problem, and I mean *any* problem, twenty-four hours a day, I want you to call me."

"We appreciate your support, Coach," Mr. Olsen said.

Coach went on to give a slightly different version of the speech he'd given to the principal about us all being "partners" and offering them tickets to every game. They seemed as impressed as the principal had been. Again, no surprise. He did impress everybody he came in contact with. He always knew what to say. I listened closely, trying to find a clue that he was just giving them a line, "playing" them, but I couldn't. You couldn't help believing what he was saying because he really did say it like he believed it. The important part was that *they* believed him . . . or even more, believed *in* him.

CHAPTER FOURTEEN

We pulled up to the Wendy's restaurant.

"Josh, go get us some food. Four number-one combos," Coach said. "And take Jake with you."

"Why don't we just use the drive-through window?" Jake suggested.

"Because I don't want to drive while I eat . . . if that's okay with you!" His whole tone and expression had changed in an instant, from pleasant to angry.

"Sure, of course," Jake mumbled.

"Good, then get us our food . . . pronto!"

Josh and Jake jumped out of the car.

As soon as they were out of earshot, Coach said, "I think we need to talk."

I didn't know if I *could* talk. I couldn't even look at him. I felt like I could hardly breathe.

"Or maybe you just have to listen and I need to talk."

I could listen. I could maybe even understand.

"I know you're pretty confused about what happened last night."

I nodded ever so slightly, still not able to look up.

"You know that you're special to me . . . with some people there's just more of a connection . . . a closeness," he said, his voice barely a whisper. He placed a hand on my shoulder and my stomach did a flip. I tried to pull away, but he tightened his grip—I was held in place, shocked by his power. "I knew I could trust you not to tell anybody," he said. "Like you didn't tell anybody today."

"But . . . but why me?" I asked, my voice barely audible.

"I told you. You're special, and with my help you're going to become even more special." He loosened his grip but kept his hand on my shoulder. "You'll be my confidant. You'll be taken into my deepest trust, and you'll have control over things. Take Jake," he said. He gestured toward the front window of the restaurant, where we could see Jake and Josh standing in line. "Like I told you, if you want, he's gone."

"Please don't do that."

"Then because you don't want him traded, he stays, just like that. I'm the coach. I can trade him or keep him. Or . . . I can simply *destroy* him. I can sit him on the bench, ride him, ridicule him, until he quits, and then I'll make sure that no other team will waste time on him. I can do that."

I knew he could. He could destroy Jake. Or anybody else on the team.

"Well, what do you want me to do with him? Are you sure you want him on the team?"

I looked at Jake. He was inside, joking with Josh. I didn't like him, but I didn't hate him.

"I told you, he can stay."

"Good answer, but it was nothing less than what I'd expect from a future captain of mine. You're putting the team ahead of yourself. You know, over the years, I've selected a few young men . . . you're not the first . . . but you are the *only* one . . . right now." He paused. "You even met one of them—at the Leafs game. He's one of your favourite players."

"You mean that Brad Simmons was . . . ?"

He smiled. "He was my special friend then, the way you are now. I did for him what I want to do for you. I want to help you to become a professional hockey player. Isn't that what you want too?"

"Of course."

"I'm going to make that all happen. I'm going to invest in you all of the time you need, give you all the opportunities, coach you, teach you. You'll become the captain, but you'll become so much *more* than that."

"But what does that have to do with what you did . . . what you did . . . to me?"

"It's about your transformation into a *man*. This has been going on forever. A great man takes a young boy as his protege and turns him into a man. This has been happening since the beginning of time, and it still happens today . . . much more than you'd think . . . it's just that nobody talks about it because some people wouldn't understand. And that's why you can't tell anybody. Do you understand?"

I didn't answer.

"I'm trusting you to keep *our* secret. Besides, if you *did* tell, nobody would believe you. It would be your word against mine."

I looked up at him. He was right. Nobody would believe me. I knew it and he knew it.

"All that you'd do if you tried to tell is destroy your future. Nobody would ever take a chance on you again. You'd be blacklisted. You'd be nothing . . . you'd become *nothing*. It would be awful for you to throw away all that you could become, to lose your future, which is so bright."

He stared directly at me until my eyes dropped to the ground.

"But, but, I'm not gay," I stammered.

"Of course you're not. And neither am I. I just have *needs*. We all have needs." He took a deep breath. "Cody, you'll learn that sometimes you have to be prepared to give a little to get a lot. I'm prepared to give you *everything*. You'll get so much more than you'll be giving and—"

The back doors popped open and Josh and Jake climbed in. Coach released my arm.

"Here's your food."

"Thanks, boys."

Jake handed me a bag.

"Thanks," I mumbled. I just didn't know if I could eat... or hold it down if I did.

CHAPTER FIFTEEN

Okay, everybody, bring it in!" Coach yelled.

The drill stopped and all of the players started to glide toward centre ice, where he was standing. I didn't glide; I skated, so I'd be in the first row.

Coach was flanked by his assistant coaches and by Terry. Terry was a hands-on owner—well, part owner—and he'd been around, on and off, for the whole second week of training camp. I wanted to show him that I understood what Coach was drilling into us about practising the way you expect to play, so I was working hard.

I knew that a bunch of the other players had already noticed how I was doing things. Some of them weren't that impressed. They saw me as showing them up. I *was* trying to show them up. That was the way it had to be. I could be friendly enough with them, but that didn't make them my friends. Teammates were just *temporary*, pretend friends who you shared time and space with—as long as you were on the same team. If any of them got traded to another team, I'd hate them with the same intensity I hated everybody else on every other team. Besides, they were also my competition—for time on the power play, ice time, and ultimately to make it to the next level.

For a whole bunch of them practice was just work and they weren't prepared to put in the time. I was. Practice was where you put "money in the bank" to draw on when you needed it during a game. Then again, some of them were just playing out the string. They weren't going anywhere after Junior. But I was . . . if I worked hard enough and listened to what I was supposed to do.

What was also becoming obvious—I'd heard a couple of the veterans grumbling—was that Coach was treating me well, saying nice things about my play. I just wanted them to see the connection—that he was treating me well because of what I was doing on the ice . . . and not anything else. I lived in fear of somebody finding out what was still happening.

I'd come to dread his apartment. The smells in the hallway, the curtains taped down, the feeling of the bed sagging, the sound of the springs, the—I pushed it all out of my mind.

"This has been a good end to a good week," Coach said. "I'm impressed with the efforts of everybody here. We all know that leadership is important. We have it, beginning with our owners." He nodded in Terry's direction.

"Just doing my job," Terry said and gave a slight bow.

"And I'm going to give that from the bench," Coach added. "But we are so lucky that we are also going to get that effort on the ice. You have a veteran—a fourth-year returning player—as your captain. Let's hear it for Steve."

We cheered, hit our sticks against the ice and boards, and the closest couple of players gave him a slap on the back. I didn't know him well, but he seemed like a good enough guy. I guess once the season started I'd see if he was a good captain.

"Our two assistant captains from last year are both gone—one ran out of Junior eligibility and the other, as you all know, was selected by the Islanders and is playing for their farm team in Portland."

There was another chorus of cheers.

"And so we have to name two new assistants. One of them is an obvious choice." He paused. "Let's have a round of applause for Owen!"

Owen was a third-year player—a good team player—and he was popular with everybody.

Coach tossed a sweater to Owen. He held it up. On the back was his name, and when he turned it around, there was a big "A" stitched onto the front. Owen dropped his gloves to the ice and pulled the sweater on. He was practically beaming.

"And the second assistant might be a surprise to some of you," Terry said. "But it's part of our goal to build a winning team, not just for a year, but year after year." He held up a second sweater, with a big "A" on the left. He turned it around and my name was on the back!

"Cody, this is for you . . . congratulations."

There was a slight pause, and then the players cheered—although it wasn't nearly as loud as the other cheers, and I noticed the looks I got from some of the older players. As I skated forward to get the sweater, I couldn't help but notice that some of them were clapping with their hands but hating with their eyes. Josh and Jake were different—they weren't just clapping, they were screaming and hooting. Jake slapped me on the back. He seemed genuinely happy for me. I'd learned to like him. He was an idiot but he was no threat. I was glad I hadn't gotten him traded . . . or destroyed.

I pulled on the sweater. It felt good. I was used to being either the captain or the assistant on every team I'd ever been on, and Coach had promised that I'd eventually be the captain, but this was a real surprise . . . or payoff . . . part of the deal.

"Okay, everybody, hit the showers," Coach said. "Except our captain and two assistants."

We stood there and waited until the ice had cleared. This meant there wasn't going to be any hot water by the time we got there. That was fine. It would give me an excuse not to have a shower until I got home. I'd become increasingly anxious sharing a shower with everybody. I really liked my privacy at home.

"Men," Terry said, "I need you to know that we are proud of what you three will bring to the team. Steve, you know how much I think of you as a player and a person."

"It's mutual, sir."

"And Owen, this is something that you've earned through your play over the last two years. Well-deserved."

"Thanks," he said. He was actually blushing.

"And finally, Cody, let me offer my congratulations on being the only first-year player who has *ever* been asked to wear an "A" on his uniform. This is a real testament to who we think you are and who you will become."

"I won't let you down, sir."

"Okay, boys, you can all hit the showers," Coach said.

I started to skate away.

"Cody, could you wait a second?" Terry asked.

The other two guys gave me a sideways glance and then skated away.

"And Coach, you go too," Terry said.

Coach looked hesitant for a moment before his usual confident expression returned. He gave me a solemn look and then nodded before skating away. I read into that brief exchange a message: *Remember, not a word.*

"Cody, I want you to know that I fully supported Coach when he suggested you become an assistant. He's not just a good friend, I also trust his judgment. I just had to be honest with you and say I'm a little worried," he said.

"I'll do my best, sir."

"I know you will. I'm just concerned about the extra pressure this will put on you. It's hard enough to break into the league without having expectations of leadership. Can you handle that?"

"I'll try, sir."

"I want you to rely on Steve as a role model, because you know that you've been earmarked to carry the "C" on your sweater someday."

"Yes, sir, I'll learn from him."

"And if the pressure gets to be too much, I want you to remember that alcohol is a problem and not a solution."

"I know, sir." I also knew that if he'd had his way, I wouldn't have been there at all, because I would have been drafted by another team.

"Do you still have my card?" he asked.

"Yes, sir." I knew exactly where it was. Not that I'd ever call him.

"Good. Twenty-four seven, just remember I'm there."

He put a hand on my shoulder and I felt a rush of fear. Could I trust him? If Coach was his good friend, was he also . . . ? How could I trust anybody? That made it even worse. There was nobody to trust and nobody to tell.

Besides, what was the point? Instead, right there in my hands was the sweater with the big "A" on the front. That was how I'd ultimately get away and into the Show.

CHAPTER SIXTEEN

Really, I'm getting enough to eat," I said to my mother over the phone. We talked a couple of times a week.

"I just worry about you."

"I know you worry."

"And I just wish I could meet the people you're staying with," she said.

"I'm sure they'd like to meet you too."

"It's just so far away. I guess talking on the phone is all we can do for now. They sound so friendly and nice. It makes me happy to know that you have a family there."

"Yeah, a family," I repeated.

They *were* a family. They just weren't *my* family. They were good, and the boys weren't bratty or anything, and the baby didn't cry too much. Of course, the boys both wanted to be in the NHL when they grew up, so we always gave them our old sticks, and the Olsens were at practically every home game.

What I had to remember, though, was that, in the end, this was just business. They were being paid to provide me with a place to live and meals to eat. It was a business deal. Sure, they were nice, but they were just employees of the team—a team that was run by Coach. He talked to them all the time. They all seemed to get along well. No surprise there. Everybody liked Coach. Everybody trusted him.

That just made me feel even more trapped. I *hated* that feeling . . . trapped like an animal. I kept trying to look for an escape, an out, a way to end it, and there was none. Well, there was one way out, but I had to force that thought away—it was too terrible, too *final.* Besides, there was no way I'd ever do that. It wasn't me. I knew I could hurt somebody else, but I couldn't believe that I could ever, for even a second, have thoughts of harming myself . . . it was just not possible . . . there was no way I'd ever do that to myself.

What if I just told him it *had* to stop? If I just said no? I'd promise not to tell anybody. I could keep it secret. Maybe that would be enough to stop it from happening anymore. What could he do if I told him to . . . ? Slowly I shook my head. I knew there were lots of things he could do. I'd seen him lose his temper. I knew what he could do to anybody on the team if he wanted.

"Cody, are you still there?"

"What?"

"I was talking and you weren't answering. I thought the line went dead."

"I guess I was just thinking."

"I was saying how much I'm looking forward to seeing you next month when Watertown plays against Toronto."

"It'll be great to see you too."

"Your dad is here now and he wants to speak to you."

"I've really got to—"

"I'll pass the phone to him," she said.

Great. I couldn't think of one thing he'd have to say that I wanted to hear.

"Cody, this is your dad."

Yeah, I sort of recognized the voice. "Hey."

"I've been following your team. Not the best year so far."

"We're in third place," I said defensively.

"And do you think that's good enough?" he asked.

"No, sir," I answered, although I wanted to say it was a hell of a lot better than eighth place, which was where the team had finished last year without me.

"And you could be doing a lot better yourself. You're not even in the top twenty in scoring."

"I'm third in rookie scoring for the whole league."

"I guess that's something. Are you being respectful to Coach? Are you doing what he's telling you to do?"

"Of course." Thank God my father, and everybody else, didn't know all of what he *was* telling me to do—*making* me do.

"You gotta treat your Coach with more respect even than you treat your old man," he said.

That was easy enough to do since I had absolutely *no* respect for my father. Maybe I didn't understand why Coach was doing it, but at least I was getting something back. There was at least going to be a payoff at the end.

"I'm going to pass the phone back to your mother," he said. "She wants to keep talking to you."

"Sure, okay . . . bye."

He didn't ask about school or how I was doing or anything except hockey. At least there was no temptation to try to tell him anything. What a laugh, even thinking about that. He wouldn't have believed me any more than anybody else would.

"Hello again," my mother said. "It's just so good to talk to you, to hear your voice."

"It's good to talk to you too."

"I know it's silly, but I'm a mother so I worry all the time about how you're doing."

"It's not silly." There was a knock on the door. "Hang on, Mom. Come in."

Mrs. Olsen poked her head in. "You have to leave for your tutoring session or you'll be late."

"I'm on the phone with my mother so I guess I'm going to—"

"I'll let you go, because it's important you don't miss that," my mother said—clearly she'd overheard.

"No, really, it's okay," I said to her. "I can miss a session or two."

Mrs. Olsen frowned.

"No, you shouldn't do that," my mother said. "Coach is going out of his way to help, and you should be so grateful. We all are. You say hello to him from us. He's such a wonderful man! I'll talk to you later. Love you."

"Yeah, you too," I said, and she was gone.

I slipped the phone into my pocket. "We're going to talk later," I explained.

"It is important to go," Mrs. Olsen said. That look of concern crossed her face again. "You really don't like to go for tutoring, do you?"

I shook my head. If only she knew how much, and why.

"You probably figure you spend enough time in school as it is. I guess you'd rather be hanging out with your buddies or playing video games or watching TV or whatever."

Whatever would be better. Anything would be better.

"But if you think about it, you boys all miss so much school because of travel and games that you're still not spending as much time in school as regular students do."

"I guess you're right," I mumbled.

"And it is obvious the tutoring is working. Your marks have all been good, and I've noticed you studying around the house."

"I've been trying hard." Part of trying hard was getting my marks up enough that nobody would think I needed to be tutored. It wasn't like he was really helping me with my schoolwork when I went over to his apartment.

"Then just think of this as an extension of trying hard," she said. "It's like they say: 'No pain, no gain.'"

I knew about the pain. I could only hope for the gain.

She gave me a hug. "You're a very good boy. Your parents must be proud of you. I know your coach must think well of you . . . giving up his time to tutor you is such a big commitment."

I didn't know what to say. I just knew what I couldn't say. "I'd better get going." I grabbed my coat and started to leave.

"What subject are you being tutored in tonight?" Mrs. Olsen asked.

"Um . . . math, I think."

"Then you might want to take that along," she said, pointing at my math textbook sitting on the dresser.

"Yeah, thanks . . . would have been stupid to forget that."

I grabbed the book. It was like adding insult to injury—lugging a book that would never be opened.

"And, Cody . . . straight home afterwards . . . no stopping . . . and nothing to drink."

I nodded. I'd overheard her and Mr. Olsen making quiet comments about me smelling of alcohol. Little did she know that I *was* coming straight home from his apartment, and the only drinking I ever did was there at Coach's. I guess I could not drink . . . no . . . I *needed* to drink.

· · ·

I walked slowly. I felt as if everybody was watching me as I passed. It wasn't that I was being paranoid. Some of them *were* watching me. The Junior A players were as close as they got to celebrities in Watertown, so we were pretty well-known by everybody. Hardly a day went by that somebody didn't mention something about the last game or ask for an autograph. That made it even worse. I lived in constant fear that somehow they'd find out. And the longer it went on, the better the chance that somebody would. I had to stop it. This time I would say something. I just had to stand firm.

I felt such a deep sense of doom, and the paranoid thoughts got stronger. I stopped in front of the building and took a long look around. So what if somebody saw me going into the building? I had a legitimate reason to be there. But I took one more glance over my shoulder as I pulled open the front door.

As I climbed the stairs, my legs felt weak and tired and shaky. Not just from giving everything I had at the practice and at school. Not just because my sleep was so screwed up. It was so much more than that.

I stopped in front of his apartment door. If I just stood there, maybe time would freeze. Maybe the floor would swallow me and—the door swung open.

"You're late."

"Just a couple of minutes," I said apologetically.

"Would you say that to me if this was a practice? Would you say that to a ref at the start of a game?"

"No, sir."

He turned around and I followed him in. "Grab a beer."

I went to the fridge and pulled out a bottle. I wouldn't have more than a couple—I didn't want Mrs. Olsen to get any more suspicious, but I needed to drink something.

"Come and have a seat," he said as he patted the couch beside him.

Usually he waited until I'd had a few beers. Waiting for it was almost as bad as having it happen. What if it didn't have to happen at all?

"I'm really having trouble with my math," I said. I held the book up in front of me, using it as both proof and a shield.

"Maybe afterwards I can help you a little."

"How about now . . . instead of?"

His eyes hardened and I felt a sense of dread course through my body. What was he going to say or do now? Then his expression softened and a small smile appeared, and I felt a chill go up my spine. He had different types of smiles. I'd learned to tell them apart. This one was smug, like something was going on that he was proud of, something that gave him an advantage.

"What do you think about Taylor?" he asked. His voice was calm and casual.

"What?"

"Taylor, your teammate, what do you think of him?"

What did he mean? Was he doing this with Taylor as well, and he wanted to let me know that there was somebody else and he was going to leave me alone?

"Do you think he's a good player?" Coach asked.

"He's . . . he's okay," I stammered.

"That's your opinion, he's *okay*. What do you think of him as a player?"

"Um . . . he's got skills. He scored some goals for us."

"Seventeen goals. Third on the team."

"But most of those are on the power play," I noted.

"Eleven of them have come with the man advantage. And his defence?" Coach asked.

"What defence? He's a minus-nine. He seems to skate a lot faster when he's trying to score than when he's trying to defend. He doesn't even try to win the battles in the corners."

"That's almost identical to what I've written in his file," Coach said. He reached down and took a manila file folder from a few that were piled on the coffee table.

"Why are you asking me about Taylor?"

"I'm thinking about trading him," Coach said.

"Who are you trading him for?"

"They're offering me a choice of two players." He handed me two files.

I opened up one and then the other. There were notes in Coach's handwriting and a picture of each player. I recognized them both.

"They're pretty good."

"And they're both two years younger than Taylor. This other team thinks Taylor would be the missing piece to push them over the top this year, so they're willing to trade away part of their future. Which of the two would you trade for?"

I studied his notes and thought about the three games we'd played against the team.

"He's got better straight skills," I said, pointing to one. "But him," I said, tapping the second picture. "I just *hate* playing against him."

"That's a big compliment . . . it's something people say about you. So, which one would you take?" Coach asked.

"If he was on my team, I wouldn't have to play against him, and the other team would hate playing against him."

"Then it's decided. I'll pull the trigger on the trade tomorrow."

"Really? Just like that?"

"Just like that. I trust your instincts. Taylor is gone, and that means you're going to be starting first unit on the power play."

"Amazing!"

"I want you to be showcased, to offer you more opportunity to impress the people you need to impress to move to the next level."

"Thank you . . . thank you so much," I said, and then I had another thought. "I was wondering . . . these files, do you have one on everybody in the league?"

"Not everybody in the whole league."

"But you do have a file for everybody on our team, right?" I asked.

"Everybody except you," he said.

"You don't have a file on me?"

"No, for you I have *two* files."

"Why do you have two?"

He gave that same dangerous smile. I felt my throat close up and sweat start to run down my side.

He got up and went over to his filing cabinet. He fingered through the files and pulled out two, holding one above his head.

"This is the one that I hope someday to show to the scouts who might draft you into the NHL." He held up the second. "And this is the one I hope nobody will *ever* have to see."

"I don't understand."

Again with that smile. "Right here I've made extensive notes about how you make the other boys uncomfortable because you stare at them in the showers."

"What?" I gasped. "Who said that?"

"And how you made sexual advances to another boy during a road trip."

"That never happened!" I exclaimed.

"And how on September 21 you came to talk to me about your sexual orientation and how I counselled you, wanted you to go and see a therapist." He ran his finger down the page. "Or here, on October 15, you threatened that you'd tell everybody that I made advances on you unless I gave you more ice time and put you on the power play on a regular shift. And, of course, that was just before I started you on the second unit of the power play. People could check the game stats and see that that really happened."

"None of that ever happened! None of it!"

"And today I'm going to write about how you made me trade away Taylor so you could get more ice time."

"I'm not making you do anything! Why would you write those things? Why would you . . ." I let the sentence trail off. I knew why.

"I have to protect myself." He paused. "After all I've done for you, you walk in here today and think you can tell me what we're going to do and not do."

"I was just—"

"Shut up and listen!" he snapped. "You don't talk, you don't think, you just listen. Do you understand?"

"Yes, sir."

"This file is my evidence. If anybody saw this, they would see the pattern, the same way they look at your behaviour from before . . . at school, on the ice, at the hockey camp. Do you want to read everything I wrote?" He held out the file.

I shook my head and drew in my hands. I didn't want to read it. I didn't even want to *touch* it.

"If I can't trust you, maybe it is time I told everybody what you've done and show them this file and—"

"No, please don't!"

"I've trusted you with my deepest secrets, and you want to betray me!"

"I don't, I *won't*, honestly!"

The smile returned, but he didn't answer right away. "I'm not going to. You can trust me to keep *our* secret." He placed his hand on my leg. "You know how special you are to me. Do you really think I'd want to do something to hurt you?"

I didn't answer.

"Well, do you?"

"No . . . of course not."

"I didn't make this file just for my protection. It's for *your* protection too," he said.

"How does it protect me?"

"By putting an end to any possibility of you deciding to talk. And you should know that it's more than just these notes. You know, I have other players up here all the time."

Was he doing to them what he was doing to me?

"And none of them would ever say I did anything but what a coach *should* do," he said. "I've shared rooms with both Josh and Jake, and they'll swear that everything was completely on the up and up, because it was. And that's the truth."

The tightness in my chest got even worse.

"Who do you think people will believe, me or you?"

There was no question—it was him.

"And with this file, if anybody had even the faintest flicker of belief that you were telling the truth, well, that belief would be washed away. You'd be over."

My whole body started to shake. He was right. He was always right.

"But there's one more thing you have to know, Cody. If you did tell, and somehow somebody actually did believe you, it would still destroy your life . . . as well as my life. And then I'd have no choice. I'd have to kill you."

"What?"

"I would kill you." He said the words so calmly, in such a matter-of-fact way. "Do you believe me?"

I nodded. I did believe him.

He smiled, and his eyes changed again—a change I'd seen so many times before. "Go to the bedroom . . . I'll be there in a minute."

I wanted to fight, argue, run away, strike out and hit him. But there was nothing I could do. I walked toward the bedroom and lay down on the bed.

He had me trapped even more completely than I'd believed possible. What he was doing was evil and awful and, in a twisted way, brilliant. But what else did I expect from Coach? He was the smartest person I'd ever met.

I heard the chain on the door as he locked us in and the world out. My stomach started churning. I closed my eyes as tightly as I could. I tried to think of other things, other places, tried desperately to let my mind escape my body, to pretend that I wasn't here and that it wasn't going to happen and—the bed sagged and the springs sounded as he climbed onto it. And then his hands were on me.

CHAPTER SEVENTEEN

The ice stretched out endlessly. Flat and white and perfect. Unmarked, untouched, unused, and pure. My legs pumped faster and faster, the skates moving quicker and quicker. The only sounds were the wind through my hair and my skates hissing against the ice. I'd never moved this fast before—nobody had ever skated this fast before. It felt more like flying than skating. I was free, and nobody could ever catch me, no matter how hard they tried.

And then I heard a new sound—somebody was coming up behind me. I dug in deeper, skated even faster, but the sound was getting louder, the person was gaining. I wanted to look behind me, but that would only slow me down. I had to keep going, but instead I felt myself slowing. The ice under my blades was melting, and I was sinking in. First my feet and then my ankles and my knees sank beneath the surface. It was getting darker, the light fading until I was engulfed in darkness. I strained to get my breath but I couldn't. It was like I was suffocating, being buried alive, sinking further and further into the ice until—

I sat bolt upright in bed, unable to stop the scream in my chest from escaping from my mouth.

A light came on and I woke up—shocked, surprised, disoriented, not knowing where I was or what was happening.

"Are you okay?" It was Josh.

"Um . . . fine," I lied—not very convincingly. My heart was practically pounding through my chest and I could feel the sweat running down my face. I wiped it with the edge of the sheet. I was in my bedroom at the Olsens' house. "Sorry for waking you."

"That's okay. I was sort of awake anyway."

It was nice of Josh to lie to me. He was my roommate for road trips. He was a good roommate—he was a good teammate, and probably the closest thing I had to a friend on the whole team. There were even a couple of times when I had fantasized about telling him what was happening, but that wouldn't have helped. He wouldn't have believed me—Coach hadn't touched him.

"Do you think I woke up Jake?" I asked.

"His light is still off. I think that guy could sleep through anything."

"Maybe *he* should be my roommate on road trips," I suggested.

"And then who would I get stuck with? No, I'll stick with you, if you don't mind," Josh said.

"That's more than fine with me, buddy. You know that."

I didn't have close friends. I guess, to be honest, I really didn't have *any* friends. I tried to convince myself that it was because it was so hard to make friends with people when you had to keep something so important from them. But really, I'd never had friends, even before. And now this awful, terrible secret was like a wall, a wedge, a canyon that separated me from everybody. Everybody except one person.

The sick, twisted truth was that the person closest to me, the person I had to trust the most, was the person doing this to me. Coach and I shared lots of secrets, including the most important one—somehow it bonded us together even more. I didn't know whether that should make me cry or laugh or scream out loud. It was pathetic, but that didn't make it any less true.

"I always find it hard to sleep after a game," Josh said.

"*You*? Funny, I had trouble getting to sleep earlier tonight because of *your* snoring."

"The guy who was screaming shouldn't be complaining about somebody else snoring," Josh suggested.

"You've got a point there."

"That *was* a good game."

"Any game we win is a good game."

"How's the jaw?" Josh asked.

I reached up and touched it. "Still a little sore."

"He really clocked you."

"I got in a shot or two." I shrugged.

"That guy is as big as a house," Josh said.

"And about as smart, but it's not like I had a choice who I was going to fight. He ran Owen into the boards and I was the closest man to him. You would have done the same thing."

"I'm not so sure about that. You're fearless . . . except maybe in your dreams. Was that guy coming at you in your sleep? That would have made me scream!"

"I'm not afraid of him."

"Then he must have punched you so hard your brain got scrambled. If you're not afraid of him, then you're not very bright."

"You go to school with me, so you know that being bright isn't one of my strengths," I joked.

"You do okay in school. You're working hard . . . all those extra tutoring sessions with Coach."

I felt a sudden jolt of uneasiness. Was he hinting at something? "None of that is my idea."

"Yeah, Coach can be pretty insistent. He's a good coach and I like him . . . but I really wouldn't want to get on his bad side. We've both seen what can happen when he gets mad." We'd all seen his outbursts. Tossing that newspaper box onto the truck had only been the first. "Not that you have to worry about that."

"What's that supposed to mean?" I felt a jolt of anger replacing the uneasiness.

"You know . . . he really likes you."

"He likes you too!" I snapped.

"Yeah, he does treat me pretty good. Jake too. Maybe it's because we're the guys he brought in, you know, his draft picks."

I felt a rush of contradictory feelings and thoughts. I should have just been glad that Josh felt he treated other people well too, but I did want him to treat me the best.

"That's probably it," I said, glad to have an escape.

"I just know he gets scary when he loses his temper," Josh said. "A couple of times, I thought he was going to climb right over the boards to get at a ref or another coach."

More and more I was starting to think that he wasn't actually losing his cool. That it was all on purpose, for show.

"But I guess you'd know better than anybody," Josh said. "I think you're the person he's closest to."

Again, getting too close. My defences kicked in. "He has lots of friends. It's like he knows everybody in hockey."

"He *is* incredible that way," Josh agreed. "I just meant you know him better than anybody on the team."

"What about Terry? They're good friends," I argued. "I know they spend a lot of time together."

"I guess so. I mean the players."

Did Josh know? Was he playing dumb, or fishing for

details, or just screwing around with me? And if he knew, did other guys on the team know, and—?

"But really, let's be honest, you do work the hardest. You're paying your dues, like you did in the game tonight. I'd be shocked if Coach didn't make you captain next year."

"No guarantees."

"You can be *my* captain *any* day," Josh said.

"Thanks. I appreciate that." I *really* did. But if he knew the truth, would he still want me as his captain, or even a teammate? "Maybe we should get back to sleep," I suggested.

Josh nodded. He reached over and turned off the lights, throwing my room into darkness. "How about if I try not to snore and you try not to scream so we can both get some sleep."

"Deal. Big game coming up," I said.

"And then there's a big party after—that's what I'm really resting up for. You are going, right?"

"Have I ever missed a game?" I joked.

"Games, no, parties, yes. You should come to this one for sure."

"No promises. My parents are coming to the game, so I'm going to see them after. I even got permission to sleep at home, so you won't have to worry about me disturbing your sleep for at least one night."

"Yeah, but you can still spend a little time partying with your teammates, right? You *need* to come to the party. It's your duty."

"My *duty*?"

"Isn't that what assistant captains are supposed to do, improve team unity?" I heard him chuckling. "Unless, of course, you're not willing to take one for the team, and by one, I mean a beer and a babe. I hear there's going to be plenty of both there."

"When you put it that way, I guess I have no choice. The sacrifices I'm willing to make for my team have no limits."

"You're the man," Josh joked.

"Can I go to sleep *now*?"

"Yes, sir, assistant captain, sir." He left my room to return to his.

I pulled the blankets up. Tomorrow, I figured, I would join them after the game and then go home and sleep, and I'd see my parents in the morning. It would be good to spend time with the guys. Sometimes it seemed like it was only on the road trips that I had that chance at all. In Watertown there just wasn't time. Between school and practices and games and, well . . . other things . . .

I pulled the pillow over my head. It would block out Josh's snoring from the next room . . . and maybe muffle my screams. Actually, there was no way I was going to get back to sleep. The only thing working harder than my heart was my head. I kept thinking about what would happen if people ever found out. It would be the end of hockey, the end of any dream I'd ever had of making it, the end of my life. I'd just disappear.

The end . . . that thought rolled around in my head once again. Before all of this, I never would have believed I could even think that way. And those thoughts were coming more often. Somehow they were almost comforting. And that scared me more than anything . . . well . . . almost anything. I was beginning to think it would be better to die with this secret than live with the truth getting out.

CHAPTER EIGHTEEN

The puck got dumped deep into the far corner. I held up, waiting for it to be cleared up the boards on my side. The forechecker went hard and the defenceman reacted, throwing it around to his partner as our centre pressed down on him. He chipped the puck but didn't get much on it, so it went right onto my stick! Both defencemen were still low in the corners. There was nobody between me and the net. I cut right out front, alone, just me and the goalie, and shot—the puck went up, past his outstretched glove hand, and rang off the crossbar and then up into the screen!

"Damn!" I screamed, smacking my stick against the boards. We needed that goal. Down by one with less than five minutes to go. I *had* to pot that one.

"Nice shot," one of their defencemen said as he skated by me. "Open path to the net and you couldn't put it in."

"Funny, I didn't have that problem with your mother last night," I said. "Of course, that net isn't nearly as big as her—"

He smacked his stick against the side of my helmet, knocking me down to the ice, and then jumped on top of me. I didn't have time to recover and I rolled over, protecting my head with my gloves as he pummelled me, and then I felt a series of thuds as players piled on top, pushing and punching and yelling. Instinctively I kept my neck and face covered up so that I didn't get nicked by any of the dozen skate blades that were all around me. I waited until enough players were pulled off to let me get to my feet. My "friend" was being restrained by a ref and he started screaming at me again.

I blew him a kiss. "Give that to your mother for me. I really enjoyed getting to know her *so* well!"

His face got redder and he struggled to get away from the ref, who had his arms pinned behind his back. I wasn't going to fight him—not now. He was going to the penalty box and we were going to the power play. This game wasn't over yet. We'd meet again in another game, and I knew we'd dance with each other for sure. I'd give him that much satisfaction.

• • •

There's no place happier than a dressing room after a win. I hadn't scored the winning goal, or even the one that tied it up with less than thirty seconds left in the game. I hadn't even been on the ice for either of them, but everybody in the room knew who'd got an unofficial assist on both goals—who'd won the game for us. Me. If I hadn't chirped the guy, he wouldn't have ended up with a double minor and we wouldn't have gone to the power play and scored to begin with.

There was lots of laughter and good-natured yelling as people flicked each other with towels, squirted water at each other, and insulted each other's body parts. It was all typical dressing room stuff. It flowed around me, but I wasn't part of it. People had learned that my game face didn't come off until well after the game.

I finished washing up and got out of the shower, a towel wrapped around me—not talking, not laughing, not looking. I couldn't help thinking about that fake file—I didn't want to *ever* let anybody think that I was looking at guys in the showers.

I went over to my locker and continued to towel off. I wanted to get dressed and out quickly so I could talk to my parents for a while and still get to the party. I wanted a beer. No, I *needed* a beer—or three or five or seven.

It had gotten to be more of something I needed to wind down, to turn my mind off. Sleep wasn't even an escape anymore. Either I couldn't get to sleep or I couldn't stay asleep, and even when I did drift off, my mind was filled with bad dreams and thoughts. It seemed like it was only after I'd had a few beers in me that I was able to relax, forget about things, and not worry.

And tonight, I *deserved* something to drink. I was a hero and I wanted to celebrate. It would be good to feel like I was part of something, part of a team. For a little while, fuelled by some beer, I could pretend that everything was okay, that these were my friends.

Josh had told me that it was a private party—an "unofficial" party at a club—and we'd been promised kegs of beer, lots of food, and plenty of puck-bunnies. I think I needed to be around a girl almost as much as I needed something to drink.

I'd dated a bit in Watertown, nothing steady. Not that I was looking for something steady, but it was important that the guys on the team see me with girls. I couldn't afford to let any rumours get started. Other guys on the team had girlfriends—somehow they found enough time. But Coach was always warning me not to let any girl get in the way of my dreams . . . or maybe it was in the way of his dream.

There was this one time, after a game, when he saw me talking to a girl and he marched over and said some things, and it was really strange. It was almost like he was jealous. How sick was that? How sick was all of this?

I needed a girl tonight. Maybe even more than for everybody else, I needed to be around girls to prove something to myself. I *wasn't* gay. I was straight. I *did* like girls. No matter what was being done to me.

Sometimes it was hard *not* to question that. Was that the reason why I'd never had a steady girlfriend? Was it because, deep down inside, I wasn't aimed that way? Was that what Coach saw in me in the first place? Was that why he chose me instead of somebody else, because he knew that I wanted to—no, that was stupid! I liked girls. I liked them a lot. I liked looking at them, being with them. I had posters on the walls in my room and copies of *Penthouse* stuffed under my mattress. Tonight I'd find a girl and show everybody what sort of man I was.

There was an explosion of laughter and screams, and I looked over. Sean was standing in the middle of a giant powdery cloud with a blow-dryer in his hand. Looked like somebody had loaded the blow-dryer with baby powder, and when he turned it on it shot out and covered him from head to foot.

Practical jokes were just a part of the locker room, whether it was filling somebody's gloves with shaving cream, or nailing their shoes to the floor, or hiding their clothes. I was okay with the pranks, but I didn't do them myself, and strangely, nobody did them to me. I was grateful for that. And, at the same time, kind of sad. That's what teammates did to each other. That's what friends did. I was sitting in a crowded dressing room filled with people, and I was by myself.

· · ·

I staggered out of the party and into the night. The cold air felt good, and as the door shut behind me, the music and voices were almost blocked and it was close to quiet . . . although there was a ringing in my ears. I wasn't sure if that was from the loud volume or the shot I'd taken at the end of the game. That guy really *had* tried to take my head off. Not that I could blame him. I would have wanted to do the same if he'd said something like that about my mother. The difference was that I wouldn't have done it. Not then, not in a way that would have hurt my team. I would have picked my spot, waited for the ref to turn around, or even waited a game or two. You couldn't let people get under your skin that way. At least, you couldn't let them see that they'd gotten under your skin. There was a difference between people thinking you were crazy and actually being crazy. Coach had drilled it into me that I needed to stay in control—the way he stayed in control. Even his temper outbursts were planned. Most people didn't know that, but I was sure of it now.

My head *did* hurt where that guy had smacked me, but it was worth it. I'd trade a wound for a win any day, and, like my father had said, there really wasn't much up there to damage. A few good shots might even settle down my thoughts. I wouldn't have minded having some things driven right out of my head.

The door opened up again, and Josh and Jake, followed by Owen and Steve, stumbled out, singing and yelling and laughing. Owen was as drunk as I'd ever seen him, and if it hadn't been for Steve holding him up, he would have fallen flat on his face.

"Here, take him," Steve said as he passed Owen over to Jake and Josh. Neither of them seemed too steady on their feet either, and for a second I thought all three might topple over like semi-drunk dominoes.

"I have to go back and clear everybody else out. It's getting close to curfew," Steve said.

"I'll help," I offered.

He opened the door and we were hit by a wave of music and smoke that practically blew us backwards. I took another deep breath of cold air and then we went back into the room. It was dark and loud and crowded and hot. There had to be over a hundred people, and their body heat alone was suffocating, the smell of sweat and beer overwhelming.

"Some of the guys aren't going to be happy to leave," Steve yelled in my ear. "Tell 'em it's orders, from *me*."

"Yes, Captain!" I said and gave him a salute. He smiled and saluted back.

The first person I saw was Kevin. He was in the corner getting "busy" with a girl. The way they were going at it, they needed to get themselves a room. Kevin was big and tough, the team enforcer. He had a couple of inches and thirty pounds on me. I'd seen him fight enough to know he could handle himself. He had virtually no chance of making the Show, but the little chance he had involved beating people with his fists, not beating the goalie with his shots. He could be difficult even when he was sober and not otherwise distracted. And it didn't help me any that he was a veteran—a fourth-year player—who probably thought I was wearing the "A" that should have been on his sweater. It would be better for Steve to talk to him.

I tapped one of our other players—Jeremy—on the back.

"Cody!" he yelled, and he gave me a big hug. "You are the man! You won that one for us, buddy!"

"Team game and a team win," I replied.

Jeremy was obviously well into the bag. I didn't think there was one person in the room who wasn't at least a little tipsy, and the guys on our team were leading in that department.

"It's time to go," I said above the noise. "Or we'll miss curfew."

"Okay, sure." He turned to the girls he was standing with. "Did you two get to meet Cody?" he yelled.

They both nodded. Not only had I met them, I'd danced with both and gotten one of their numbers—although for the life of me I couldn't remember either of their names. After the sixth or seventh beer, everything had started blurring together. I wasn't feeling any pain myself.

"You're going to call me, right?" one of the girls asked me.

"Count on it." I just hoped she'd written her name on the slip of paper or I wouldn't know who to ask for if I did ring the number.

She reached over, grabbed me, pulled me toward her, and gave me a long kiss good night. I was so shocked that I almost pulled away, but I didn't. That wouldn't have looked good. I needed to put on a show. I bent her back over and kissed her long and hard for good measure. Jeremy hooted and gave me a slap on the back so hard that I almost chomped down on her tongue.

I stopped the kiss, but kept one arm around her waist. She was pretty, happy, and very drunk. Too bad we needed to go.

"Next time I'm in town," I said.

The puck-bunny's smile got even bigger. Jeremy hooted again. He looked very impressed. That was even more important than what *she* thought of me. I might never see her again.

"They're waiting for you out there!" I yelled at Jeremy, pointing at the door.

He nodded, gave the other girl a big kiss, and headed out, threading his way through the crowd. He bumped into some of the other guys going in the same direction. I rounded up a couple more and even enlisted Tanner— who seemed remarkably sober—to help get the others. It didn't take long.

"Do you see anybody else?" Steve asked.

"Did you get Kevin?" I yelled back.

"I didn't even see him. I thought he was out already!"

I looked through the crowd and into the corner. He was there in the dark, partially hidden, still intertwined with that girl. I pointed, and Steve craned his neck until he could see him too.

"Go and get him and I'll meet you outside. If we don't get them moving soon, we'll lose a couple of them!"

What could I do? The captain had asked me. I pushed my way back into the room toward Kevin. He was way too occupied to notice me until I was practically on top of them.

I tapped him on the shoulder. He turned around and glared at me.

"I'm a little busy here, rookie," he snapped.

"We have to go."

"*You* have to go." He turned away, back to his business.

I reached out and grabbed his arm, and he suddenly spun around and gave me a push away. I staggered backwards.

"Screw off!" he yelled.

He took a couple of steps toward me. His fists were clenched. He was ready to fight me, right there and then. It was strange, but now that he was reacting the way I thought he might, it was more comforting than disturbing. I liked to predict what was going to happen, even if that prediction got me a shot in the teeth.

I didn't think I could take him, not straight-up and not without getting the jump on him. Still, if we'd been on the ice, I'd have had no choice but to answer the bell and fight him. I shook my head slowly. This *wasn't* the ice and I didn't have to fight him. I didn't care if a couple of dozen guys and puck-bunnies were watching, waiting for us to put on a show. What he didn't know was that I didn't *care* if he came or not. It wasn't me who was going to get into trouble.

"We all have to leave, but you stay if you want!" I yelled over the music.

I turned and walked away, half expecting him to reach out and grab me and spin me around. I balled my fist . . . waiting. With each step, I felt a little more relaxed—no, I couldn't allow myself to relax.

I pushed through the door. Maybe he'd get back in time for curfew. Maybe he wouldn't. None of it was *my* problem. It just felt good to get outside again, although it wasn't so quiet anymore. A bunch of drunken hockey players were combining for a loud chorus of singing, swearing, and yelling.

"Where's Kevin?" Steve yelled over the noise.

"He's decided he's going to stay."

"That's not his decision to—"

The door burst open and loud music and Kevin spilled out. He didn't look happy. He stomped toward me. "Who do you think you are to order me around?" he screamed.

"I was—"

"You think because you're Coach's little pet you can tell me what to do, you stupid puke?" he screamed.

"I wasn't trying to—"

He pushed me hard, propelling me backwards, almost knocking me off my feet. He came forward, fists raised. This was going to end in a fight whether I wanted it or not.

Steve stepped in between us.

"*I* asked him to help me get everybody so nobody would get in trouble. You got a problem with *me* telling you what to do?" Steve demanded.

Kevin looked like he wanted a scrap. Was he really stupid enough to pick a fight with our captain?

He lowered his fists. He relaxed and turned toward Steve and away from me. This was over.

"Okay . . . fine . . . as long as it isn't *him* telling me what to do," Kevin said, pointing at me. "I'm not going to take any guff from that little suck-up. He's practically the coach's girlfriend."

I charged him, bowling him over! When we hit the ground, I drove my head right into his face and I heard something snap!

All of a sudden there were hands all over me, pulling me off. As they lifted me by my arms, my legs were still free and I kicked Kevin right in the face! He screamed out in pain. As they hauled me away, I was still trying to get a final kick in.

"Let me go!" I yelled.

They all held me firm.

"Okay, okay . . ." I stopped struggling.

"Let him go," Steve ordered, and they released me.

Kevin had been hauled to his feet by a couple of the guys. He was still being steadied by one of them. Blood was pouring from his face and he was in obvious pain.

"This isn't over," he snarled.

"Why, are *you* going to rat me out to Coach that I kicked *your* butt?" I demanded.

"You little—"

"I'm big enough to take care of you!" I snapped, cutting him off.

"You just wait until—"

"Why do I have to wait? Am I waiting for you to grow some balls?" I yelled. "I'm here right now. Come on!"

I took a step toward him and I saw it—he cringed slightly. He was afraid. I had to put him down right now while he was—

"That's it!" Steve yelled as he stepped between us again. "This is over. Unless you want to take a run at me too."

He looked directly at me. He had seen the same thing in Kevin that I'd seen.

I held up my hands. "I didn't start it." But I had finished it.

He turned to Kevin. "Do you want to fight me?"

Kevin didn't answer right away. He tried to glare at Steve, but it didn't come off through the blood and pain. He lowered his eyes and nodded. "I'm okay . . . it's over."

"Good. Now both of you, shake hands."

Slowly, reluctantly, we stepped forward. I extended my hand but had the other one balled up, ready to swing at him if he tried to hit me.

He gave me a crooked smile. "That was a pretty nice shot, kid."

"Sorry about the girl. I didn't mean to interrupt."

"Her? Nothing special there. Just a puck-bunny," he said. "You better remember, kid, I'm expecting you to have my back the next time I'm in a brawl on the ice."

"You can count on it."

We shook hands and he threw an arm around my shoulders and practically pulled me off my feet as he gave me a big hug.

"That's more like it," Steve said. "Now we better get back to the hotel before curfew." He looked at me. "Wait, you're not staying with us tonight, are you?"

I shook my head. "I'm home for the night, but Coach made it clear that I have the same curfew, only at my house."

"Just be back at the hotel in time for the bus. We leave at eleven."

"I'll be there at ten-thirty."

"We'll see you then."

Steve shook my hand and then Kevin gave me another big hug. To anybody who wasn't a hockey player, that might have been shocking, but that was the way it was. One minute trying to take off somebody's head, and the next all forgotten and forgiven. Other players slapped me on the back and basically everybody yelled out a good night. They started off, one big, loud, intoxicated parade, walking toward the hotel.

I stood there watching, feeling sad that I wasn't going with them, but realizing that even if I was, I still wouldn't be part of them. I turned and walked away. Their shouting and laughter echoed off the building, fading as we moved in different directions, until finally I couldn't hear anything. It was quiet, and I was alone.

CHAPTER NINETEEN

I moved as quickly as I could. It was cold and the wind was cutting, and no matter which way I turned, it still seemed to be blowing straight into my face. I looked at my watch. It was just after twelve-thirty, so technically I was now late for curfew. Not that my parents even knew that I had a team curfew. But what if the next time they talked to Coach, they casually mentioned to him what time I got home? I knew they still talked to him on the phone sometimes. Well, there was nothing I could do about it now. And I wasn't going to be that late. It was only a couple more streets.

I stepped onto the road and a car whooshed past, almost hitting me! I jumped backwards as my heart jumped up into my throat!

The driver blared his horn as he sped off into the night. I hadn't seen or heard him at all. I'd been too inside my head. Another step and he would have hit me. That was too close—or maybe not close enough. If he had hit me, what would have happened? He would have killed me, or maybe just hurt me so badly that I couldn't play hockey. Either way, that would have been okay.

That thought sent a shudder throughout my entire body. I felt scared. The fact that these thoughts were coming more regularly was even scarier. Not that I wanted to die. I didn't. I really didn't. I just wanted a way out. If the car had just winged me, I'd still be alive but not able to play.

Part of the reason I was fearless in the game was that I almost hoped to be hurt, injured so badly that I'd have to go home to finish out the season. I couldn't believe how, in a few short months, hockey had gone from being my refuge from the world to just another place of pain. At least if something had happened, I'd have had an excuse to either quit hockey or quit life, and nobody would have questioned why—it would have looked like an accident. I could almost hear what people would say.

"Cody was drunk . . . probably tripped or fell into the car . . . you know he had a problem with alcohol, just like his father."

I could picture the funeral service. It would probably take place in Watertown. The whole team would be there, all of them in their jerseys. I'd be in mine too, lying there peacefully in my coffin. They'd probably put in my stick, maybe some trophies I'd won over the years. There would be lots of flowers, and the church would be overflowing with people from the town and from my school. Maybe that puck-bunny would even be there crying—what was her name? Leslie . . . Lisa? It didn't matter. Her crying would be part of it, and anybody who had any doubts would know that I was straight.

My parents would be sitting right up front. My mother would be in tears. My father would be half in the bag, and everybody would just excuse him because of what had happened and how hard he was taking it because he loved me so much. What a joke. But at least it was something he could use for an excuse for the rest of his life to explain what a drunk he was.

Everybody would have good things to say about me. Whether they meant them or not, it didn't matter. Who had anything bad to say about the dead? Even players from the other teams would say nice things. Each team from the league would send a representative—a coach or manager, maybe even a player or two. And then, when everybody was gathered, there'd be a eulogy. I didn't have to guess who would give it.

Coach would go on and on about what a wonderful player I'd been and how tragic it was that my life had been cut so short. What he wouldn't say was that he was the one who ended it. Even though he wasn't driving the car, he'd have been the one who threw me under the wheels.

Would he feel bad about it, or would he even know that it was because of him that I was dead? Probably not, but what did it matter? It would be over for me.

I couldn't help but wonder how long it would be before he found somebody new, somebody "special." I knew I wasn't the first, and whether I died or not, I wouldn't be the last.

I stopped in my tracks and took a deep breath. That thought seemed to bother me more than thinking about my own death. Who was he going to do this to next? Who else was going to have to go through what I was going through? But why should I care? Nobody had cared enough to step forward and stop it from happening to me.

I heard another car coming. It was moving quickly, and standing there in the dark, I was sure that the driver hadn't even noticed me yet. I was practically invisible. All I had to do was throw myself in front of him. It would be over in just a few seconds. He was getting closer and closer and—I took another step back and let him race by. I couldn't let it end like that. *I couldn't.* The only choice I had was to keep going. Put up with it. Get through it.

I was more than halfway through the first season. Then I'd be safe at home for the summer. It was the first time I'd ever thought of my home as safe. After that there'd be two more seasons, maybe a third, but it would end, and then I'd be free, in the NHL, where he couldn't reach me, or bother me, or touch me. The only way to beat him was to just use *him* the way he was using me. I'd take his advice as a coach, let him play me, talk to people for me, and then finally be free. There was no other choice. I wasn't going to step in front of a car because of him.

I crossed and hurried down the street—down my street. I'd lived here most of my years, but somehow it all seemed strange. None of it had changed. *I* was the difference. I wasn't the same person I'd been just a few months ago. Had it really only been a few months? It seemed like forever.

I came up to our house and stopped on the sidewalk. There were still lights on. I hadn't expected my mother to go to bed before I got home, because she never did. I could only hope that my father was "asleep"—the word my mother always used for him passing out on the couch.

The house certainly hadn't changed. It had the same broken-down furniture on the porch, still missing the same spindles, with the same semi-broken-down piece of crap car in the driveway. The sidewalk was shovelled. I guessed my father had made my mother get out and do it. He never shovelled it himself—you know, "bad back."

I just stood there, staring at my house. All I'd ever wanted was to leave . . . and now . . . all I wanted to do was walk in that door and go to my room and close the door behind me. Sure, my father would give me some grief, but there was nothing he could throw at me that I couldn't handle.

"I'm home!" I called out as I walked in.

"Yes, you are."

It was Coach!

"And it's fifteen minutes after curfew."

CHAPTER TWENTY

"**Y**ou thought that because you're at home you don't have to pay attention to curfew?" Coach asked.

"I . . . I . . . no . . . of course . . . I'm just . . ."

Coach started laughing and my mother and father came out of the kitchen. My father was laughing like crazy and my mother had a nervous little smile.

"I'm just giving you a hard time," Coach laughed. He came over and put his arm around me. My whole body went rigid. "We were just having a beer," he said. He led me into the kitchen. "Sit."

I sat down at the kitchen table, and Coach sat beside me. My father sat opposite us. I did a quick count. There was almost a case of empties on the counter.

"What are you doing here?" I asked Coach.

"Is that any way to speak to your Coach?" my father snapped. "You come in late and I can smell the alcohol from here. You've been drinking, haven't you?"

"*You're* going to lecture me on having something to drink?" I demanded.

"You think you're too big for me to give a whipping to?" my father yelled. He started to get to his feet but slumped back over, too drunk to even stand up.

"Hey, hey, hey!" Coach said, looking right at my father. "No fighting, no arguments. So he had a beer or two. Are you telling me you didn't have more than a few when you were his age?"

"Well . . ."

"My guess is that by the time you were sixteen, you could drink most grown men under the table. Am I right or what?" Coach questioned.

My father smiled. "I could always hold my own." He sounded so *proud*.

"I thought so. Then I have a suggestion." Coach reached over and grabbed a bottle of beer from the counter. He snapped off the cap and handed it to me. "I think you two should stop fighting about beer and share a couple." He raised his bottle. "I'd like to make a toast . . . to a father and son who probably have more in common than they'd like to admit."

We tipped back our bottles. All right, I could drink without agreeing with what I was drinking to. Truth was, I didn't have anything in common with him except a last name, and the thought that we shared even that made me feel like I could use another drink.

"Isn't that better?" Coach asked. "And in answer to your original question, I just came over to pay my respects to your parents and they insisted that I stay for a meal and a drink."

"He's a pretty good guy, this coach of yours," my father said. "Only thing I can't understand is what he thinks is so good about you!" My father laughed—a loud, raspy, drunken laugh.

"You saw what I like during the game. He had himself quite a game tonight," Coach said.

"Tonight?" my father questioned. "I didn't see him light up the net."

"If he hadn't drawn those penalties, we couldn't have won," Coach said.

"You mean when he turned turtle and let that guy pound on him?" my father said. "I never turned turtle in my whole life!"

"If I hadn't—"

Coach reached out and grabbed my arm. "Let me," he said. Then he turned to my father. "I can't agree with you more. It's important to answer the bell."

"Damn right!" my father snapped.

"But doing what you have to do to win is more important. If he'd fought back, he would have drawn a roughing penalty as well, and we wouldn't have had the four-minute advantage," Coach explained. "Without that advantage, we wouldn't have scored and we wouldn't have won. Sometimes you have to know when to take one for the team. He took one for the team." He paused. "And speaking of the team, after the game, did everybody have a good time tonight?"

"I think so."

"And they're all back at the hotel?" Coach asked.

"They were heading there when I left them. I'm sure they made it on time. Steve rounded everybody up . . . with help from me."

"A good assistant always helps his captain."

"I try. Would anybody mind if I went to bed?" I asked. "I'm really tired."

"Um . . . I made a bed up for you in the basement," my mother said.

"The basement? Why can't I sleep in my room?"

"Coach is staying in your room," she said.

"What? You're staying with us?"

Coach smiled that smile and I felt a chill go through my body.

"He wanted to leave but we *insisted*," my mother said. "We couldn't let him leave after he'd had something to drink."

"And we sure as hell weren't going to put *him* in the basement!" my father thundered. "After all he's done for you, the least you can do is give up your room for a night!"

"Look, I don't want to put Cody out. I can take a taxi back to the hotel. It's no problem," Coach said.

"It's a problem for us," my father exclaimed.

"We'll have none of that," my mother added. "You are our guest and you will be staying."

"Then I could stay in the basement," he offered.

"No, you won't. You're staying in Cody's room," my father said. "Kid should show a little gratitude, a little common courtesy. I thought I raised you better than that!"

"I'll only stay if it's okay with Cody," Coach said.

He was asking my permission, like I could possibly say no, like I even remotely had a choice.

"Yeah, sure, of course." I stood up. "I have to get to bed. Mom, can you wake me up by eight? Good night, everybody."

My mother gave me a big hug and walked me out of the room, her arm still around my waist, leaving the two of them behind in the kitchen, laughing and talking.

"I'll be waking you with pancakes," my mother said.

"Chocolate chip?"

She smiled. "Of course." She gave me another big hug. "I missed you."

"Me too, Mom. Sleep well."

• • •

This certainly wasn't the first time I'd slept down in the basement. In the summer, when it got hot upstairs, it was always cool down there. But year round it was the best place in the house to get away from my father yelling and my mother crying.

I shifted around on the little cot. I was so looking forward to spending just one night in my own bed. And instead of me, *he* was in it. It seemed so *wrong*. Would it ever feel the same again to be in my room, in my bed?

Down deep I knew why he was at the house. No matter what he said about trusting me, he really didn't. He was making sure that I didn't talk to my parents. But he needn't have worried. I wasn't going to tell them. There was no point. I knew who they trusted more, who they would believe, and even who they liked more. I was second in every category.

I heard a sound and turned over. I caught a glimpse of movement. Was it my mother, or—

"Cody?" It was Coach. "Where are you?" he called out.

What was he doing down here? Oh no . . . it couldn't be that . . . it couldn't. I sat up.

"Cody, don't make me yell. You wouldn't want me to wake up your parents. Where are you?"

"I'm over here," I said quietly.

He turned toward me and slowly moved in my direction. He sat down on the edge of the cot and it sagged under his weight.

"Your parents are both asleep. Or more like passed out, in your father's case. I could hear him snoring. Do you know why I'm down here?"

I knew. I just couldn't believe it.

· · ·

I sat at the table watching my mother and Coach talking and laughing while they made breakfast together—bacon and eggs, French toast, coffee, and, of course, chocolate chip pancakes. This was all so unreal. I couldn't believe any of it. As much as I wanted to eat, I wasn't so certain that I'd be able to keep it down. I felt sick to my stomach.

My father was still asleep. I hadn't been able to sleep for more than a few minutes all night.

"So, are you hungry?" Coach asked.

For a second I didn't realize that he was talking to me.

"Sure, yeah . . . it all smells really good."

"It's almost ready. You'd better wake up your husband," Coach said to my mother.

"I'll be right back," she said.

He used a flipper to lift the pancakes off the grill and onto a plate. He put it on the table right in front of me. "Do you know why I came here last night?"

I nodded. "I wasn't going to tell them." There was no point. Not even my parents could stop him. Nobody could.

"Good boy. You are a good boy."

CHAPTER TWENTY-ONE

I sat with my head in my hands, wondering what was going to happen next, talking to nobody, looking at nobody, as kids streamed in and out of the school office. This wasn't my first trip to the principal's office, but so far I'd done nothing bad enough to get me suspended. At least until now.

It had all happened so fast. One second I'm sitting in class, half asleep, half hungover, completely lost, not paying any attention to what the teacher's saying. The next he's calling on me, and then calling me *out* in front of everybody about some stupid assignment I'd forgotten I even had, and one thing led to another until I told him to screw off. And that, of course, had brought me to my spot on the bench in the office, waiting for Mr. Paisley to see me. And waiting . . . and waiting.

I guess I really shouldn't have been complaining about the time. More time gave me more opportunity to cool down. By then, having sat there for the better part of two periods, I was pretty calm. If he'd taken me in right away, I probably would have told Mr. Paisley to screw off as well.

"Cody."

I looked up. One of the secretaries was standing at the counter looking at me. "Mr. Paisley will see you now."

I got to my feet. I knew that I had to apologize, fast and sincerely. I'd heard about students being suspended for swearing at teachers, and I did not want to be suspended. I'd got close a couple of times this year—missed assignments, sleeping in, skipping some classes, and a couple of times they'd suspected that I'd been drinking. Of course, I *had* been drinking, because I'd been drinking more and more as the year went on. I just said the smell was my aftershave or my mouthwash. It wasn't like they could give me a Breathalyzer. Unfortunately, I'd had a couple of beers that morning. I knew it wasn't going to have any effect on me, but sometimes it stayed on my breath even after I'd brushed my teeth.

The door to his office was open and I walked in and—"Terry!" I exclaimed.

There was a second door to the principal's office and he must have come in that way, where I couldn't see him enter. He got up from the couch and came over and shook my hand. "Are you okay?" he asked.

I shook my head. "I guess I'll find out how bad it is," I mumbled.

"I tried to get in touch with Coach Connors," Mr. Paisley said, "but he wasn't available."

"He's out on a scouting trip," Terry explained. "They passed the call on to me."

"Thanks for being here," I said. "I really appreciate it." I did appreciate it. He was a big deal in town. He had an even better chance than Coach did of rescuing me.

"No problem, son. Let's just try to sort things out," Terry said.

"I've explained to Terry why you were sent to my office this morning," Mr. Paisley said.

"And I really want to apologize," I said. "To you and to Mr. Griffin. I had no right to say any of that."

"I appreciate you saying that," Mr. Paisley said. "And you'll certainly have an opportunity to offer your apology to Mr. Griffin personally. I'm just concerned about this whole pattern of behaviour."

"As am I," Terry said. "I had no idea there were ongoing issues."

"We've been keeping Coach Connors informed with each incident," Mr. Paisley said.

"I'm sure you have. I don't doubt any of what you've told me. I just wish I'd been informed myself." He paused. "I'm particularly worried about the reports that you've come to school under the influence of alcohol on a number of occasions."

"They have no proof of that," I protested.

"Proof?" Terry asked.

"I mean . . . I wasn't drinking."

He looked at me—he looked right *through* me. I just didn't feel like lying anymore. I knew he wouldn't believe it anyway.

"And today?" Terry asked. "I know *somebody* in this room has been drinking, and it isn't Mr. Paisley, and it hasn't been me for years. Well?"

I shrugged. "I had a couple of beers this morning to calm my nerves."

"Thank you for being honest," Terry said. "I know that wasn't easy." He turned to Mr. Paisley. "Do you think I could have a few minutes alone with Cody?"

"Of course!" Mr. Paisley said, getting to his feet. "You can use my office. I'll be right outside." He closed the door behind him.

"Cody, I want to ask you something, and I want you to be completely honest with me," Terry said. "Can you do that?"

I nodded. "I can try."

"Trying isn't enough. Can you be honest, yes or no?"

"I can be honest, sir."

"I'm counting on it. How often are you drinking?"

"Not that much," I said. "Really."

"I didn't ask how much. I asked how often. Is it every day?"

"Not every day."

"But most?" he asked.

Once again I nodded.

"Do you think you have a problem with alcohol?"

"It's just that I need it sometimes so that I can—" I stopped myself in time before I said too much.

"So that you can what?" he asked.

My mind raced, looking for an answer, a lie, something to stop him from finding out the truth. But all I could come up with *was* the truth.

"I drink to forget."

"But it doesn't work, does it?" he asked.

"No, sir. It doesn't make it go away or stop me from thinking about it."

"Whatever the problem is, alcohol only pushes it away for a few minutes or a few hours, and then it all comes back, stronger and worse than ever," Terry said. "I know what you're going through."

He thought he knew, but he didn't. I wasn't just drinking because my dad was a drinker.

"We all have our reasons, our excuses. All alcoholics do. Do you know what your reason is?" he asked.

I shrugged again.

"Do you want to talk about it?"

I took a deep breath. "I can't."

How could he ever understand what had happened to me? He was a former NHL player, a tough guy, and I'd been . . . been . . . I felt myself start to shake. I fought hard to keep the tears that were just inside from getting out.

He got off his chair and knelt down in front of me, so that even though I was looking down at the floor, I couldn't help but look at him as well.

"Whatever it is, we can fix it. I just feel bad that Coach Connors isn't here and you have to rely on me to take care of things."

I shuddered. How could I tell him what was wrong when he thought Coach was the *answer* and not the problem? "You wouldn't believe me even if I told you," I whispered.

"Son, there was a time fifteen years ago when somebody didn't just believe *me*, they believed *in* me and helped me. I'm here to return that favour." He paused. "I know you're putting everything on the line. So, whatever it is, whatever you say, I'll believe you. You have my word."

I started crying, tears exploding, my chest throbbing, deep, uncontrollable sobs, so loud that I knew the staff and students waiting outside in the office couldn't help but hear me. I didn't care and, more than that, I couldn't have controlled myself even if I did.

"It's all right, son, it's going to be all right," Terry said. "I know this isn't easy, but it all starts right now. One step at a time, and the first one is the hardest. Do you know what you want to say?"

"I know," I sobbed. "I just . . . just . . . don't know if I can."

"It takes strength to break free. I know you have the strength."

If he really meant it, if I told him and he believed me, it would all be over. Not just what Coach was doing to me, but my whole future would be gone. It would be over. No more dreams. Nothing. I'd be nothing. Even if he did believe me, I'd have thrown away everything. But, like he said, maybe, just maybe, I could be free.

CHAPTER TWENTY-TWO

The dressing room got quieter as each player finished packing up his gear, said his goodbyes, and
left. The end of the season always had a sadness about it
as everybody headed off in their separate directions. The
next year would be the same but different, because some
of the people wouldn't be back and new people would
take their places. It was amazing how a group of indi-
viduals could come together as a team, and then, when
it was over, it was over. All that was left would be some
memories and a team picture. This year I didn't want to
keep either.

I sat at my stall. I was packed but in no rush to leave.
Here in the dressing room was where I felt most comfortable. During those first half-dozen games after the news

came out, even the ice wasn't a refuge. Though there was a publicity ban on my name, everybody knew.

Terry sat down beside me. "You almost ready to go?"

"Sure . . . I was just thinking."

"Lots to think about . . . for all of us."

Josh walked over. "Thanks for everything," he said as he and Terry shook hands.

"Thank you for a great season. I'm just sorry you had such a lousy coach to finish up the year," Terry told him.

"You're a good coach!" Josh protested.

"No need to suck up to the coach anymore. My time is over. We've got you a *real* coach for next year."

Terry had been our coach for the last third of the season and through a second-round exit in the playoffs.

"So we're going to get together this summer, right?" Josh said to me.

"Count on it."

"You sure you don't need a drive home?" Josh asked. "My parents are waiting for me and there's definitely room for you and your stuff in the car. Think of it as one more road trip together."

"Thanks, but I'm okay. Terry is going to drive me home."

"Oh . . . I understand."

Understand . . . I didn't know if anybody really did. Some of them tried. Others didn't. But who could blame them? It had happened to *me* and I still didn't understand it all myself.

"I was heading down to the city on business anyway, so it will be nice to have company on a long drive," Terry explained.

Josh reached out and we shook hands. "I just want you to know that . . . you know . . . if there's anything I can do . . . *ever* . . . you know that . . . right?"

"I know."

"You and me," he said, pointing back and forth. "Brothers."

"As long as you realize I'm the tough big brother."

"No argument there. Okay, my parents are waiting. We'll talk."

He left us alone, the dressing room now empty except for me and Terry.

Terry sighed. "I like dressing rooms. I'm going to miss this next year."

"You're the owner. You can still coach if you want," I said.

"I'm the owner and that's why I'm *not* going to coach. I have to protect my investment." He smiled. "Besides, you boys deserve more than I can give you. Don't worry, I got you somebody you can trust."

There was no need to say anything more.

"So, you're going to see Josh over the summer," he said. "He's a great guy. The whole team has been good, haven't they?"

"Pretty good."

"It must have been hard out there, though," he said.

I knew he meant the rink. "The first game back was the hardest."

I'd missed three games after it all came out. And it was incredibly hard getting back on the ice knowing that everybody in the arena was looking, thousands of pairs of eyes all on me, questioning, wondering, gawking, thinking.

At least I couldn't hear what they might be saying to each other. On the ice, I couldn't avoid the comments from some of our opponents—taunting me, trying to get under my skin. They were just doing to me what I probably would have done to them if the tables had been turned. When somebody saw a weakness, they had to try to exploit it to help their team win. If they'd found out I had a sore hand, they would have slashed me there. It was the same thing. It still hurt, but I couldn't let them see it. I just had to play harder, dig deeper. And I did. And I did and I did, until finally the ice became my sanctuary again, the place where I felt safe. Coach couldn't get to me and what he'd done couldn't get to me. It could only make me stronger.

"I want to thank you for everything," I said to Terry.

"It was the least I could do. After all, it was my fault."

"Your fault?"

"I'm the one who hired him. I'm the one who didn't see what was happening."

"Nobody saw."

"But I should have. I just hope you'll forgive me for not seeing it. At least he's going to get what's coming to him," Terry said. "And I'll be there right beside you at the sentencing."

That was still three weeks away, and I'd been trying to block it out of my mind until after the season was over. Now that it *was* over, I knew it would dominate my thoughts.

Originally we'd been told there was going to be a trial—months and months, maybe even a year away—it didn't seem real. And then suddenly Coach had just pleaded guilty and admitted it all. No trial. No testimony. I had been preparing for a battle, him using the phony file on me, dragging me through the mud, but he just caved in. He was nothing more than a bully in a fancy suit with fancy words, and most bullies don't have the guts for a fight. I should have been grateful, but it was almost like I'd been cheated out of a chance to say how I felt, to finally face him and win. In the end he'd cheated me out of that.

Some people thought he did it to be "kind," so nobody would have to go through a trial. I knew that kindness had nothing to do with it. After the news broke—after the initial shock and disbelief had worn off—three more of his former players had come forward. Their stories were almost identical to mine. The police said there might even be a whole lot of others who'd had the same thing happen to them but didn't have the guts to come forward. Was that what it was, guts? Or was it just desperation?

"You're not going to be alone. It's not just me, but the

other boys—the men—he's assaulted. Because of you they came forward. Because of you he's never going to be able to hurt anybody else."

I was so relieved when the first person did come forward—when it wasn't just my word against his. Still, I had to admit that at first I was angry. If that guy had said something a long time ago, I wouldn't have had to go through any of this. I tried to understand. Nobody knew better than me how hard it was to talk, but he should have, all of them should have. Then again, if somebody else had broken the news first, would I have come forward to testify? Maybe, maybe not. I really didn't know. I was working hard to put the anger away, but it wasn't easy.

The team had arranged for me to see a therapist. That was the last thing in the world I wanted to do—tell someone else, another stranger, all about it, live through it again—but they basically forced me to do it. I was glad they did. It helped—it helped with the anger.

Funny, the anger had been with me so long that I was almost afraid to lose it. If I wasn't angry, what would I have? I wondered if I'd be able to play with the same intensity if I wasn't fuelled by rage. But I discovered that I could. It wasn't the anger that was driving me now, it was the desire.

"We'd better get going," Terry said.

I got up and slung my hockey bag on my shoulder. My suitcase was already packed and in Terry's car. We walked out of the dressing room. He closed and then locked the door behind us. I felt a sudden rush of relief. The season was over. It was over.

We walked out to his car.

"It sounds like your parents are helping you through all of this," Terry said.

"My mother is great, and my father . . . well . . . at first I don't think he even wanted to believe it, but really, he's a lot better than I expected . . . when he isn't talking about killing him."

"I understand that. Believe me, that thought has crossed my mind more than once. I hope your parents understand about you not being at home too much this summer."

"I'll be there long enough," I said. "Besides, I'm looking forward to camp."

"I'm looking forward to having you. You'll be a positive addition to the staff."

We climbed into the car and he went to start the engine, but I stopped him.

"I know I've said it already, but I need to say it again. Thanks for what you did for me. Everything. I couldn't have done any of this without you," I said.

"Don't ever sell yourself short," Terry said. "You helped *me* get through it. You taught me a thing or two about being tough."

"I taught you?"

"Every day. I knew you were tough out there on the

ice. I just didn't know how tough you *really* are. It took strength to do what you did. At the beginning of the season, when we made you an assistant captain, I didn't know if you could handle the pressure. Over the past months, you've handled more pressure than anybody would ever have expected. I'm so proud of you, son."

I didn't know what to say. I felt close to tears.

"Now there's just one more thing I need to ask you. You don't have to give me an answer right away. You can have as long as you want to think it over."

"What do you want me to think over?" I was suddenly feeling anxious.

"I've had calls from other general managers asking about trades, and your name has come up a number of times."

"You want to trade me?" I gasped.

"No, not me. Other teams want to trade *for* you, want you to be part of their teams. I just want to know if you want to be traded."

"Why would I want that?"

"I thought that you might like to have a fresh start, a new place, without all the memories of what happened here. If that's what you want, then I'll arrange for one of those trades. *Is* that what you want, Cody?"

"What do *you* want?" I asked.

"That isn't important."

"Yes, it is," I insisted. "Do you want to trade me to another team? Would it be better for everybody if I left?

Would it make it easier to forget this happened?"

"Son, no matter what, I will *never* forget what happened. *Never.* You have my word." He paused. "If I have my way, I'll have you sitting right here next year. The only difference will be the "C" you'll be wearing on the front of your sweater."

"You want me to be captain?"

"You've earned that right. You're a leader, a player, and most important, somebody we have all learned to respect. So . . . do *you* want to stay?"

I wanted to say that this was my place. Where I belonged. And I wasn't going to be chased away, not by that man and not by his memories. I wasn't running from this fight.

"I don't want to go anywhere," I said.

He smiled. "That's what I hoped. We'd better get going."

I knew where I was going—and not just today. I was going to make it. And nobody was going to stop me. Not even me.

AFTERWORD
By Sheldon Kennedy

Power Play, although a work of fiction, took me back to a time in my life that was very REAL—when I was sexually abused as a young hockey player by my coach. It is a book about the unbelievable fear and chaos that a young person experiences when they are hurt by a trusted adult. It's about the invisible trauma that abuse victims carry around, day in and day out. I have spent the last fifteen years trying to prevent any young person from having to write a story like this about their own life.

The damage caused by all forms of abuse, bullying, and harassment is hidden. You feel guilt, shame, self-hate, depression, anger, and helplessness—and you feel completely alone. Other injuries, like a broken leg, are easy to see, understand, and treat, but abuse victims suffer in total isolation. What makes it even worse is that abusers are often trusted adults in your community, school, or family. You don't think that anyone will ever believe that this "respected person" could be doing something so monstrous. As kids, we look up to the adults in our lives; we trust them and want to please them. That's why the abuse of power, as portrayed in *Power Play*, is so scary and unforgiveable.

When my sexual abuse became public in 1997, it was the first time that the media really paid attention to the issue as it relates to the athlete-coach relationship. Two years later, I took the opportunity to in-line skate across Canada to raise further awareness of this invisible trauma. What I learned, as did many other Canadians, was that the problem was more common than anyone had ever imagined. My goal, since then, through my work at Respect Group, has been to educate all adults working in schools, sport, and youth-serving organizations about the prevention of abuse, bullying, and harassment. If we empower our adults to be watchful for the signs of abuse and sensitive to the young people they work with, we have a better chance of preventing child sexual abuse from happening—or at a minimum, from happening over and over again.

My advice to any young person experiencing any form of abuse or bullying is to report it to a trusted adult. Just like Cody did in *Power Play*. Tell your teacher, a family member, or your coach. The sooner the better. You will not be alone, and you will be assured that it's not your fault. Because *it is not your fault!* If that seems too tough, reach out to the Kids Help Phone at **1-800-668-6868** or visit **www.kidshelpphone.ca.** They can assist you anonymously and give you the support you need.

Sheldon Kennedy skated for the Detroit Red Wings, the Calgary Flames, and the Boston Bruins during his NHL career and played for Canada's gold medal–winning team in the 1988 World Junior Hockey Championship. He is the author of Why I Didn't Say Anything, *an account of the abuse he suffered for five years at the hands of his Major Junior Hockey League coach. He continues to carry his message through Respect Group Inc., the company he co-founded.*

AUTHOR'S NOTE

My background is in teaching and social work. As a social worker, I was employed at both the Children's Aid Society and the emergency department of a hospital, and in these capacities I was involved with children who had suffered abuse. I saw situations that were terrible and tragic and real.

I drew upon my experiences and training in portraying the situations and characters in this book. I hope Cody's story will provide readers with a greater understanding of what victims of abuse go through and help victims realize that they are neither alone nor responsible—that there are people out there to help them. The first step is the hardest; it takes great courage and bravery to reach out and break free.

I am very thankful for and appreciative of the courage and dedication of Sheldon Kennedy. It is an honour to have a person of such integrity write the afterword for my book. He is a true hero.

Eric Walters